Su

A "Dete

ystery'

Mary M. Cushnie-Mansour

Saving Alora

Ordering Information:
Books can be ordered directly from the author's website: http://www.writerontherun.ca or through Amazon (direct links are on author's website) For volume order discounts, contact the author via email, mary@writerontherun.ca

Cover Art by
Jennifer Bettio

Published by
CAVERN OF DREAMS PUBLISHING
Brantford, ON, Canada

Printed and bound in Canada by
BRANT SERVICE PRESS
Brantford, ON, Canada

Also available on Amazon in print and Ebook formats

ISBN 9798638990466

What Readers Are Saying About the "Detective Toby Mysteries"

The "Detective Toby Mysteries" grab you right from the beginning and hold you in suspense until the very last word. They keep you wanting more. Delightful and exciting reads! Well Done! Mary Cushnie-Mansour is a very gifted writer!

...Mary Sass

I can't put these books down. Very intriguing and full of surprises. I thoroughly enjoy the "*Detective Toby Mysteries*" and look forward to more of Toby's adventures.

...Isobel Dobbin

The "Detective Toby Mysteries" are gripping and fast-paced, filled with suspense, detail, and drama. Masterfully written. Toby, the cat, is quite an insightful detective. I look forward to seeing where Toby leads us in the future.

...Barb

Detective Toby Mysteries are an original concept having a cat as a detective. Fun reads that are hard to put down. The stories keep you wondering what will happen next.

...Steve Hasper

Cushnie-Mansour definitely keeps the reader's attention enough to keep reading, while internally trying to guess which direction the characters will take us. Numerous surprising twists and turns definitely leave a reader wanting more. The "*Detective Toby Mysteries*" are a quick read that flow at a good pace and keep the reader turning pages to see what will happen next!

...Janna Maranda

What great books! The "Detective Toby Mysteries" are fast paced and the perfect read to bring along on a vacation. I especially love Toby! Now I am wondering what my orange tabby cat is up to when he heads out the door. I highly recommend!

...Bev Katalenas

The "Detective Toby Mysteries" are great books! I love Toby—he is an amazing cat!

...Myra Houston

I really enjoy your books. Toby is wonderful, along with a good story plot. I sure hope we will hear some more of Toby's adventures.

...Donna Fischbacher

On a rainy or snowy afternoon, find a comfortable chair, with a steaming cup of tea or coffee beside you and spend a perfectly relaxed time getting into amazingly pleasant and entertaining books. The "Detective Toby Mysteries" by author, Mary M. Cushnie-Mansour are an interesting treat for anyone.

...Mirella VanDerZyl

Everyone's favourite orange tabby, Toby, will have readers happily diving headlong into heart-stopping mysteries. Feisty, intelligent Toby is wonderfully arrogant, and with good reason. He's got a nose for solving crimes and being in the right spot at the right time. Whether he's crouched in trees, spying on the bad guys, or going for seconds at every meal, he's consistently a thorn in the side of criminals, and solidly on the side of good.
I enjoyed this series immensely, and try desperately to savour them, but end up reading ever more quickly (in between bursts of laughing out loud at Toby's unique take on the situations he finds himself in) to reach the end and find out how Toby managed to overcome the bad guys. The "Detective Toby Mysteries" are delightful cozy

mysteries sure to please ... and to keep you up late, turning pages!

...Regina Jetleb

Amazon Reviewers:

I really enjoy this detective series where the old, wonderfully arrogant tomcat, Toby, is the detective and prowls around, righting wrongs.

...LegoManiac

Great reads!
I enjoyed this series immensely—can't put them down. Toby was first introduced in "Mysteries from the Keys," a book of short stories. Cushnie-Mansour has taken Toby on bigger adventures since then, and I've enjoyed all of them.

...Judith Holliday

Suspenseful page turners! The suspense and action are high, and the endings are perfect. Highly recommend if you're looking for mystery page-turners you can't put down!

...Amazon Customer

Toby the big orange cat detective stumbles across mystery after mystery that needs his skills to solve. Mary's creative imagination keeps us on our toes while Toby works tirelessly to solve the mysteries and save lives, all while being a cat whose actions must speak the words he is unable to whisper in the ears of those around him. Mary continuously captures our attention with her great characters and creative story telling. Great reads!

...C.M. Durling

Real Thrillers! Great books ... very gripping keeps you reading. Could not put them down!!!

...Edna Malcolm

Enjoyable. Loved the books. An easy read with very different settings and characters. Unexpected turns and twists in the plots.

...H20 Dawn

Loved the characters and the stories in this series. I especially loved the twist of a big orange tabby cat as the prime detective. His voice put a new perspective on solving the mysteries, which were quite interesting to read. I would highly recommend the "Detective Toby Mysteries" by Mary M. Cushnie-Mansour.

...Amazon Customer

There is nothing not to love about this series. It is set in a local town and features a smart, fast-thinking tomcat, Toby, who lives with a retired cop. Once his belly is full, Toby has a nose for sniffing out the bad guys, and he always gets them ... one way or another!

...Amazon Customer

"Fairy tales are more than true: not because they tell us that dragons exist, but because they tell us that dragons can be beaten."
— *Neil Gaiman*,

"There is no greater agony than bearing an untold story inside you."
— *Maya Angelou*,

"When I despair, I remember that all through history the way of truth and love has always won. There have been tyrants and murderers, and for a time, they can seem invincible, but in the end, they always fall. Think of it--always."
— *Mahatma Gandhi*

Books by Mary M. Cushnie-Mansour

Night's Vampire Series

Night's Gift
Night's Children
Night's Return
Night's Temptress
Night's Betrayals
Night's Revelations

Detective Toby Series

Are You Listening to Me
Running Away From Loneliness
Past Ghosts
Saving Alora

Short Stories

From the Heart
Mysteries From the Keys

Poetry

picking up the pieces
Life's Roller Coaster
Devastations of Mankind
Shattered
Memories

Biographies

A 20th Century Portia

Youth Novels

A Story of Day & Night
The Silver Tree

Bilingual Picture Books

The Day Bo Found His Bark/Le jour où Bo trouva sa voix
Charlie Seal Meets a Fairy Seal/Charlie le phoque rencontre une fée
Charlie and the Elves/Charlie et les lutins
Jesse's Secret/Le Secret de Jesse
Teensy Weensy Spider/L'araignée Riquiqui
The Temper Tantrum/La crise de colère
Alexandra's Christmas Surprise/La surprise de Noël d'Alexandra
Curtis The Crock/Curtis le crocodile
Freddy Frog's Frolic/La gambade de Freddy la grenouille

Picture Books

The Official Tickler
The Seahorse and the Little Girl With Big Blue Eyes
Curtis the Crock
The Old Woman of the Mountain
Dragon Disarray
Bedtime Stories

Acknowledgments

I would like to thank all the fans of the “Detective Toby Series,” who, after reading the first book, asked for more ‘Toby.’ Muses come from many sources, and the initial inspiration for this series came from an old orange tabby cat sitting on a windowsill in a house in Hamilton, Ontario. As my mom and I walked past the house, there he was, staring at us. I turned to my mom and said: “I wonder what the old fellow has witnessed looking out his window?” From there, I wrote the first story about Toby—The Witness—which was a three-part short story for the *Brantford Expositor*. “Are You Listening to Me?,” “Running Away From Loneliness,” “Past Ghosts,” and now, “Saving Alora” are novels filled with the Toby’s adventures, and he is quickly becoming the favourite feline detective of readers.

My love and understanding of cats, I believe I inherited from my mom and grandmother, is echoed loud and clear in Toby’s voice. Thanks, Mom and Grandma.

Again, as always, I would like to thank my editor, Bethany Jamieson, for her edit on the final manuscript, and Cavern of Dreams Publishing for publishing yet another of my books.

Thanks to Jennifer Bettio for the cover art and other pics. She managed to capture exactly what I wanted. Adding the finishing touches to my cover is Josef Stevens from Smashing Pixels. Never to be forgotten, Randy Nickman, from Brant Service Press, for the superb printing job.

As always, last, but never least, thanks to my husband and family for their continued faith in my dream.

Detective Toby

Would like to

Dedicate

"Saving Alora"

To the

Women and children

Who are

Survivors

Of

Domestic abuse

1

Toby's heart was still bleeding from the loss of his precious Emma. He lay, disconcerted, on the back of the couch, dreaming of better times and wondering who would be moving into Emma's house. Toby closed his eyes and envisioned the first time he'd laid eyes on Emma. She was so beautiful. So kind and gentle. She'd given him special cat treats and treated him like a king, even setting aside the overgrown mutt that accompanied her around.

Of course, Emma's brother, Camden, had been another story. Toby had taken an instant dislike to him! From the moment they had crossed paths, Toby knew there was something wrong with the young man, and his cat instincts had proven right. Camden was a serial killer, and poor Emma knew nothing about his escapades—or so everyone had thought at the time. Toby knew better now, after what he'd witnessed Emma doing in her basement a few months ago. She'd gotten away with it, but that's another story.

Toby opened his eyes as the roar of a large truck engine intruded on his thoughts. *Must be the new people moving into Emma's house. Jack mentioned someone would be moving in soon.* Toby still thought of the house as Emma's.

Toby sat up and gazed out the window as a large moving van came to a stop in front of the house next door. A red Volkswagen pulled into the driveway. Toby squinted, trying to get a closer look at who his new neighbour was going to be. A young woman exited the driver's side and then opened the back door, leaned inside and assisted a little girl out.

Not impressed! A kid!

But that was just the beginning of Toby's nightmare. A dog bound out of the car! A large, white, fluffy dog! An excitable dog that jumped and danced around the woman and the child!

Toby turned away from the window as Jack entered the room. "What's up, old man?" Jack asked. "Oh, I see our new neighbours have arrived. I wonder who they are," Jack said, peeking out the window.

Toby growled. *Not anyone I care to know … well, maybe the woman if she'll give me treats. But definitely not the kid and most definitely not the dog!*

Jack snickered as he looked out the window and saw the dog in the driveway next door. "Oh, now I see the reason for your discontent—a dog!"

Not to mention the kid!

Jack grabbed his cap from a hook by the front door. "Guess I'll go introduce myself." He gazed back at Toby. "Coming, old man?"

Toby hesitated before jumping down from his perch on the back of the couch. *May as well get the introductions over with, then I won't have to bother being neighbourly afterward. Boy, do I miss my Emma. I wonder if she's okay … hopefully, she's staying out of trouble. Hard to know since she moved away and is under her brother's influence now. That can't be a good thing with him being a killer. Then again, I guess she might be too. I witnessed a different side of Emma … a character I wouldn't want to meet in a dark alley. Jack did good, hiring Jeremy Davies to defend her, but it seems I'm the only one who knows the real truth. Well, me and Emma.*

Toby's mind conjured up visions of what he'd witnessed Emma doing in her basement—torturing a young man. The fact she'd gotten away with what she'd done was like a two-edged sword that tortured Toby. But Jack had explained everything to him, detailing how Emma had a valid explanation to refute everything the cops had against her.

But I know better, Emma. I know you did it. Thank God, the guy, scumbag that he was, lived and didn't remember you or what you did to him.

Toby wasn't happy when Emma decided to move closer to her brother, a convicted murderer, not only in Brantford but on the West Coast, as well.

Didn't like the guy from the moment I laid my cat eyes on him ... good thing, too. I sensed he was up to no good, and I was the one who caught him red-handed and solved the mystery of the mysterious flu that was killing people in our town.

Jack was waiting patiently by the door. "Are you coming or not, Toby?" he asked, a little grin on the corner of his lips.

Toby flicked his tail as he made his way off the couch. By the time he and Jack arrived at the neighbour's house, Toby noticed the dog was already locked in the backyard, along with the little girl. The woman was standing by the front door, directing the movers where to put the boxes and furniture. Toby studied the new neighbour.

She seems like she might be okay, but she's not my Emma. And she has two strikes against her—a kid and a dog!

Jack walked up the steps and held out a hand: "Hi, welcome to the neighbourhood. I'm Jack, and this," Jack pointed to Toby, "is my cat, Toby. We live next door."

"Yes, I noticed you came out of that house," the woman nodded her head in the direction of Jack's house and smiled warmly. "Nice to meet you, Jack. I'm Heidi," she offered in return.

Toby noticed, despite her smile, Heidi appeared annoyed at the intrusion. *Something closed about Heidi, and I'm thinking there's more to her than a sweet little mama! I wonder where her other half is … surprised Jack hasn't asked where they are.*

After a few moments of awkward silence, Jack ran his hand through his thinning hair. "Well, I guess we'll leave you to it. Sorry to have bothered you."

"Oh … no … no bother at all … I'm just focused here on making sure things get put in the right rooms. It'll save time not having to look for things later, or having to move my furniture from one room to another…" Heidi paused and pointed to the stairs, "If you could take that trunk up there and put it in the first room on the left," she directed the young male mover.

He nodded and grimaced as he struggled with his oversized load. It was one thing to bring it from the truck and up a couple of porch steps, another to carry it up a full flight of stairs.

Jack stepped forward: "Here, let me give you a hand with that." Turning back briefly to Heidi, Jack blushed, "if that's okay with you?"

Heidi set her lips in a firm line. She didn't want extra help, especially from someone who might be a nosey neighbour, but it appeared the young man was going to have a struggle getting the trunk up the stairs on his own. She didn't want it dropped and damaged; it had belonged to her grandmother. Heidi gave an abrupt nod.

Once again, Toby noticed the tension in Heidi's facial muscles. *She doesn't want us here … I wonder why*

... what's she hiding? Toby decided that while Jack was playing the do-gooder, he would check out what was going on in the backyard. He made his way down the steps and over to the fence. The kid and the dog were lying on the grass under the old maple tree. The kid was staring up at the leaves; the dog was sleeping.

A leaf fluttered down from a low branch, heading directly to the dog's head. The kid giggled and swatted the leaf away before it could land, but in doing so, she wacked the dog on the head. Instead of the dog being upset, it wagged its tail and reached over and licked her face. Then, noticing intruding eyes peering into the yard, the furry creature stood up and barked in Toby's direction.

Toby, deciding there was nothing of any importance to him at the house next door, went home. *No need to wait for Jack; knowing him, he's going to help the movers finish their job, and then I'll have to listen to him complain about his sore muscles for a few days!*

2

Heidi stood on her front porch and watched the moving truck leave. Jack came out of the front door and shoved his hands in his pockets. "Well, guess I'll be heading home now," he said. "My old cat's probably wondering where I got to," he grinned.

"Really?" Heidi looked puzzled. "Why would he wonder?—he's just a cat."

Jack sputtered out a deep chuckle. "I'm afraid, miss, Toby is not just any cat. He's a detective cat, and if anything goes awry around here, he'll be on the job right away!"

"I see," Heidi said. "I'll have to keep that in mind. But I don't think I'll ever need your cat's help." Heidi motioned to the backyard where her daughter and dog were waiting by the gate. "My dog, Bear, will ensure no harm comes to us." She paused, then called out to her daughter. "Alora, go around to the back door; I'll let you and Bear in the house from there." Turning back to Jack, "Thank you for your assistance," she dismissed.

Jack was left standing alone on the porch as Heidi went into her house and closed the door.

Inside, Heidi leaned on the door and clenched her fists. She didn't need any nosey neighbours in her life. They would just make things worse for her and Alora. She'd taken great care to get away from her ex, even changing her first and last name. It would have been too difficult to explain a name change to her daughter, so she'd left that alone. A light knock on the back door jolted Heidi from her musings. She walked through to the kitchen and out into the three-season room.

"Sorry, love," Heidi apologized as she slid the door open.

"It's okay, mommy," Alora giggled. Then, "Me and Bear are hungry," she informed.

Heidi sighed and shrugged her shoulders. She pulled her cell phone from her pocket and scrolled the internet to find a pizza joint. Having found one that suited her taste, Heidi ordered supper.

Jack found Toby sitting by the empty cat dish. The old cat gave the owner of the house a disdainful look.

"Okay, old man … I apologize … but those movers would still be moving stuff in if I hadn't stepped in and helped out." Jack made his way over to the cupboard and pulled out a bag of cat food. "Not as if you're going to starve to death if your meal is a bit late," Jack commented as he filled Toby's dish.

That's what you think, Jack. I expend a lot of energy in the line of work I'm in!

Jack grimaced as he put the cat kibble back in the cupboard. He placed a hand on the lower part of his back. "Think I'll have a good soak in the tub before hitting the sack," he said, leaving the kitchen, making his way to the bathroom.

Bingo! I'm never wrong. I knew Jack would complain about his muscles, and now I'll have to listen to his constant moaning. Maybe I'll just hide out somewhere so I won't have to hear about all his aches and pains!

After finishing his kibbles, Toby returned to his back-of-the-couch perch and took up his vigil of the neighbourhood. Nothing much was happening—just a pizza delivery next door. Then, after a short time, darkness. Toby closed his eyes. Jack had gone straight to bed after his bath. The house was silent.

3

Heidi paced in the darkness of her room. She hadn't bothered to set up the beds, deciding instead to just sleep on the mattresses for one night. Alora had thought that would be fun, almost like camping. She was asleep shortly after her head hit the pillow.

Finally, Heidi stopped pacing and walked to the window. She looked out into the night, and her mind wandered back to a time before everything went wrong…

> Heidi had met Cain while on vacation in Cuba. He'd been there, on his own, recovering from a failed relationship, he'd told her. Heidi, herself, was trying to heal from a deep hurt—the death of her grandmother. Her friends didn't understand why she was so devastated over the death of a woman who had lived a long life—95 years. But Cain had understood. He had a grandmother whom he loved dearly as well, and Cain said he didn't know what he'd do if he lost her. She'd been his rock over the years when he was growing up. His parents were always away for something—business and pleasure. He said he thought they just didn't want to be around him, but his grandmother had told him otherwise.
>
> Heidi often wondered if Cain had made up his grandmother because she'd never actually met her. When Heidi would ask questions about his

grandmother, Cain avoided answering by changing the subject—after her life fell apart, though.

Cain wined and dined Heidi every night, and during the day, they took long walks on the beaches, taking in the beauty of the ocean and the island vegetation. By the end of the week, they'd been inseparable. They were pleased to be on the same flight home and that they didn't live too far from each other in Hamilton. When they arrived at the Toronto airport, they shared a cab home.

The next month Hiedi and Cain had several dates and even more sleepovers. It didn't matter whose place, as long as they were together. Six weeks after Heidi met Cain, he asked her to marry him. There was no hesitation in her voice when she said yes.

Heidi had been happy for the first three months. She couldn't believe how lucky she was to have landed such a man as Cain. There was only one thing that bothered her, though. Her husband was evasive about what he did for a living. Cain said he was in sales, never saying what he sold, and hadn't even told her the name of the company. Cain said it wasn't necessary to know such details when she asked, what he inferred, were too many questions. All she needed to know was there was a roof over her head, food on her table, and enough money in the bank to have anything she wanted.

When Heidi discovered she was pregnant, she didn't push the issue anymore. She was ecstatic. The life she'd dreamed about when she was a little girl was falling into place—just as her grandmother had said it would.

After announcing she was pregnant, Cain began spending more and more time on lengthy business trips. His excuse was that the company he worked for was expanding around the world and he was their best salesperson; he was the one the bosses sent in to close deals. He apologized but said he was training a new guy to help him out so that after the baby was born, he'd have more time at home.

However, that didn't happen. Cain hadn't even made it home from an overseas trip the day Alora was born. Naming her baby was purely Heidi's choice because Cain had shrugged his shoulders and told her he didn't care what she called the kid.

Life had continued to go downhill after Alora was born. Over the next few months, Heidi found herself drowning in postnatal depression. Cain had moved her to a place in the country, far removed from any friends she had, and far from any neighbour that she might walk to if she required help. He reasoned he thought the fresh country air would do her good and improve her health. That was also when he'd brought home a little white puppy.

Heidi had named the puppy Bear. She'd always been more of a cat person, but the puppy grew on her, and soon enough, Heidi began to come out of her depression. She also realized her daughter needed her, even if her husband didn't seem to.

There was a large steel barn on the piece of land Cain had purchased, and Cain spent a good deal of money winterizing the building. Once finished, he began to entertain there. Heidi had watched cars come and go and began to feel apprehensive about what she was seeing. Long black limos with shaded windows. Men in suits. Limo drivers in suits, waiting patiently by or in the vehicles. Her husband telling her she was not allowed to go in the barn or anywhere near it when he was having meetings. Or any other time, for that matter.

By this time, Alora was walking and talking. She was afraid of her father, shrinking away from him the few times he came around. Heidi couldn't blame her child for such behaviour, due to Cain's long absences, but that Cain started becoming short with their child irritated Heidi. Finally, she spoke up when he was yelling at her about Alora's lack of interest in him. She told him straight it was his fault his daughter didn't want to be near him.

That was the first time Cain slapped her. Hard. He told her to keep her mouth shut and never speak to him like that again. Heidi took a good hard look in the mirror later that night after Cain left the house. She'd noticed the dark circles around her eyes, her hollow cheeks, how thin she'd become. She'd touched the side of her face where Cain had slapped her—where the skin was still mottled red from Cain's hand—and the tears had begun to flow.

Alora had heard her mommy crying and come to the bathroom. Standing in the doorway, the child started to cry as well, bringing Heidi out of her remorse. She needed to be strong for her daughter. She needed to find a way out.

Getting away from Cain proved to be more difficult than she thought it would be. After that first incident, he began locking Heidi in the house. He cut off the house phone and took away her cell. He even went as far as getting all the groceries for the household, and when he wasn't home, he had arranged someone to deliver the food to the barn. It must have been someone he knew well, probably one of his colleagues, because they had a key to Cain's domain behind the house. He'd also removed Bear from the house, taking away something he knew Heidi loved. She'd had no idea what he'd done with the puppy, but then, one day, while looking out a second-story window, she saw someone taking Bear for a walk around the steel building.

One day, Cain came home and caught Heidi trying to jimmy one of the windows open, and by the end of the week, all the windows had bars on them. He told her it was for her safety and the protection of the kid. Cain hadn't even bothered to call her by name. As Heidi thought back on the first two years of her child's life, she couldn't recall Cain ever calling Alora by name.

Eventually, Heidi mentioned it would be nice to get outside for some fresh air, indicating Alora needed to be in nature. After all, Heidi articulated, wasn't that the reason they'd moved to the country? Cain's face had turned red, and not from embarrassment. Anger. He raised his hand, as though he was going to hit her, but then dropped it and left the room. The next day, one of his colleagues opened the back door, walked into the kitchen, and told Heidi he was there to take her and Alora for a walk outside.

Despite not wanting to be under guard while outside, Heidi obliged. Her thinking was that she might see a means of escape—something she had begun to think she had to do before Alora woke up one day without a mother. Her companion's name was Lorenzo, and the only words he spoke once they were outside were that she wasn't to go too far ahead of him. She was to stay within his sight range, and she wasn't to try anything stupid.

Heidi had begun to walk toward the large building at the back of the house. Alora ran ahead of her. "Bear!" she'd cried out, and Heidi heard barking from inside the facility. She'd turned to Lorenzo and asked him if he could bring the dog out so Alora could play with him, and to her surprise, after looking cautiously around, he agreed.

Bear jumped around excitedly upon seeing Alora and Heidi, and for the first time in weeks, Heidi laughed because of the antics of her child and the puppy. Eventually, Lorenzo said it was time to return to the house. He gathered Bear and returned him to the steel building, then led Heidi and Alora back to their prison. He told Heidi he would return every day at the same time so they could have a bit of fresh air.

One morning, three weeks after Lorenzo had started walking her and Alora, and three weeks without her husband being around, Cain showed up instead of her walking companion. Alora cringed away from her father when he reached out to brush her cheek. Heidi noticed how his face had turned red and how he clenched his fists. She'd stepped quickly between the two of them and begged him not to hurt Alora. He'd smiled, evil racing across his lips as they curled sarcastically. He hit her, sending her to the floor. And then she felt the foot in her gut—more than once. Alora was screaming, and for every scream, Cain kicked Heidi again.

A knock on the door saved Heidi. Lorenzo entered, using his key. Despite her condition, Heidi noticed the look of shock on his face at what he was witnessing. Cain stopped his assault and asked Lorenzo what he wanted. Lorenzo told him the guests had arrived and were waiting in the barn. Cain left quickly, pushing past his employee. Lorenzo made a move toward Heidi, but her husband ordered his employee to leave her alone and follow him.

Heidi managed to stand and take Alora from her highchair, trying to calm her still-crying child, despite her own pain. She'd seen how uncomfortable Lorenzo had been by what he'd witnessed, and she began to formulate a plan in her head, thinking he might be her salvation out of this place.

Making her way over to the window, Heidi watched her husband and Lorenzo walk across the backyard. Lorenzo glanced briefly back to the house. Heidi observed the number of cars parked behind her house—six. Six drivers leaning casually on the vehicles, cigarettes hanging from their mouths. Alora stirred in her mother's arms. Heidi turned away from the window, straightened her shoulders, and vowed she would find a way to escape the nightmare she'd landed herself in!

Tears running down her cheeks, Heidi turned away from her window, heading to bed. It had been a long day. It had been a long five years.

4

Toby was startled from his sleep by a sharp, annoying barking. He stretched from his couch perch and looked out the window into the early dawn. The trees across the street swung lazily in the morning breeze, sending leaves to the ground below. Fall was on its way. Toby shivered, just thinking about the snow that would soon follow.

I think arthritis is setting into these old bones ... maybe I should eat more fish ... those ads on TV keep talking about some sort of fish oil that's good for the bones.

Not having a good view of the yard next door from the living room window, Toby made his way to the kitchen and jumped up on the window sill by the sink. *Oh, great ... the fluffy white mutt is chasing squirrels this early in the morning. At least Emma's mutt was quiet when he went out for his morning constitutions!*

Toby continued watching Bear romp around the yard, barking incessantly at whatever moved. Toby couldn't see a squirrel in sight anywhere. *Hopefully, Jack's sleep will get disturbed too, and then he'll do something about this outrageous early-morning alarm clock!*

As though on cue, Jack appeared in the kitchen doorway. "What the heck is all that racket?" he mumbled, his voice hoarse with sleep.

Toby turned and looked at Jack, then, switching his tail angrily, he looked back out the window and meowed.

Jack joined his companion, leaning on the sink to take a look at the commotion going on outside. It took a lot to rustle Jack's temper, but being woke from a pleasant dream this early in the morning was enough to grate on a good man's mood. He reached over to Toby and rubbed behind the old cat's ears. "Almost makes you appreciate Emma's dog, doesn't it, old man? At least he was quiet."

My thoughts exactly. Hope you're going to talk to this new neighbour and tell her that she needs to muzzle the mutt. Toby jumped down from his perch and made his way to the food dish.

Despite being irritated at the morning disruption, Jack managed to chuckle. "It's good to see you haven't lost your appetite, old man." Jack fetched Toby's kibble bag and filled the cat dish. "Well, may as well make myself a coffee," Jack added, shuffling over to the coffee machine. "Maybe it wouldn't hurt if I broached the subject with our new neighbour about letting her dog out so early in the morning. Damn! The sun isn't even fully up yet!"

Toby took a break from eating to look up at Jack. *Good man, Jack … I knew you'd step up to the plate and deal with this issue before it gets too far out of hand.*

Heidi watched Bear romping in the backyard. She knew it was too early for him to be out, especially since he was barking up a storm, but he'd come into her room and insisted he needed to go outside. Heidi's mind wandered away for a moment, praying she'd made the right move and that Cain wouldn't be able to find her here. The last thing she needed was trouble with neighbours, and Jack seemed to be someone who would attempt to infiltrate her life in a do-gooder manner.

Lorenzo's face crossed Heidi's mind. She hoped the man was going to be okay, that Cain didn't figure out who helped his wife and child escape the prison he'd kept them in. It took a lot for Lorenzo to help her and Alora, but he wasn't able to get the image of Cain brutalizing her out of his head. He'd told Heidi that the day after it happened—when he'd come to get her for the usual morning walk. Heidi recalled the conversation…

"Are you okay, Heidi?" Lorenzo asked.

"I'm fine. Why would you care?" Heidi had replied tersely. "You're one of my husband's puppets."

"You might think so, but one thing I don't tolerate is beating on a woman or a child."

"Oh, you just tolerate having them locked up in a prison," Heidi threw in his face.

Lorenzo had reached out a hand and gently touched Heidi's cheek. He'd looked down into her eyes, his own filled with tears. Heidi pushed his hand away, not feeling she wanted to be touched by a man who was her husband's lackey, despite his apparent remorse for what his boss had done.

"I can't undo what Cain did to you, Heidi, Lorenzo began, folding his hands behind his back. "But, as I said, I don't tolerate such behaviour…"

"Why do you work for my husband?" Heidi interrupted.

"I need the money," returned the simply. "Cain pays well."

"Exactly what does Cain do?" Heidi asked.

"You don't know?" Lorenzo looked puzzled. "I thought you would have figured it out by now."

Heidi looked at Lorenzo and shook her head. "All I know is that he's a salesman of some sort. I don't even know what company he works for."

At this point, Lorenzo laughed. "Oh, he's a salesman, alright! But he doesn't work for anyone. Cain is his own boss!"

Bear's barking at the back door brought Heidi back to the present moment. She opened the door for her faithful companion. The dog clipped across the kitchen floor, heading to his dish, his tail wagging furiously. At the same time, Alora appeared at the bottom of the stairs, rubbing her eyes sleepily. She shuffled over to her mom and circled her arms around her mother's legs.

Heidi reached down and tousled her daughter's hair. "You're up early, sweetie."

"Bear woke me up, Mommy."

Heidi laughed. "He wanted out early today … I'm sorry he woke you. I'll have to keep a better eye on him when he goes out this early. All that barking probably woke up our neighbours too, and I am sure I'll hear about it later."

Alora released her mom's legs and climbed up on one of the kitchen chairs. She leaned over the table, her hands folded, a thoughtful look on her face. "The man next door has a nice kitty, Mommy … can we get a kitty?"

Heidi laughed. "What do you think Bear will think of that?"

Bear, hearing his name, looked up from his dish and wagged his tail.

"See," Alora pointed to her pet, "he'd like to have a furry friend."

"Well," Heidi didn't want to commit to anything yet, at least until she knew that she and Alora were safe. Bear was one thing, another animal to look out for and feed would be something else. The money Lorenzo had procured for her was only going to last so long. Sooner or later, Heidi was going to have to get a job. "We'll consider it, maybe, once we get settled in."

"What's for breakfast, Mommy? I'm hungry." Alora wiggled back in her chair.

"What would you like?"

"Pancakes and sausages."

Heidi sighed. "I'm not sure if I know where the pancake mix is," she said. "Why don't we just have some cereal this morning, and then you can help me start putting our stuff away. We'll have pancakes and sausages tomorrow morning. Okay?"

"Okay, Mommy."

Heidi looked at her daughter, her heart skipping a beat. She was so lucky. Alora was a malleable child, despite all that had gone on in her five short years. She never gave Heidi an issue. The terrible twos and horrible threes that Heidi heard other moms complain about before she had a child were non-existent with Alora. Heidi sometimes prayed that it wasn't because Alora observed her mother taking so much shit from the man she was supposed to call *Daddy*. Alora had learned quickly not to anger her daddy. She'd learned to accept with a smile all the gifts he would bring her when he returned from his long trips. Heidi had made sure to leave all of them behind.

5

When Toby finished his breakfast, he had an inkling to get out in the fresh air and stretch his legs. *It won't hurt to investigate next door … get the lay of the land … see if the mutt is going to be an enemy … a creature to watch out for.* Toby sauntered over to his cat door, turned and looked at Jack, who was sipping his coffee and reading the newspaper, and let out a meow.

"Heading out, old man?" Jack looked up from his morning ritual. "Going to check out the new neighbour?"

Toby flicked his tail, then disappeared into the outdoors. Making his way over to Emma's house—he still thought of the house as hers—Toby approached his spot cautiously in the fence where he used to come and go when Emma lived there. He paused, searching the yard for the mutt. Everything was quiet.

Wiggling under the opening, Toby almost didn't make it. *Must have gained a pound or two since Emma left … have to get out more. Can't have this superior cat body going to pot!* Toby darted across the lawn, heading to the back door. He noticed the three-season room was piled high with boxes.

As Toby got ready to move forward, the inside door opened, and the mutt, along with the kid, entered the room and made their way through the box maze to the back door. Toby darted under the steps, hiding just in time. Bear and Alora raced into the backyard, Alora laughing and Bear jumping excitedly.

Toby tried to figure out how he was going to get out of the yard now. *I definitely don't want to be stuck under these steps for however long these two decide to play.* No sooner was that thought out of Toby's head that Bear ran over to the steps and began barking and sniffing around.

I'm doomed!

Toby heard the door open. "Bear! What are you barking at now?" Heidi called out, sounding annoyed.

Really doomed!

Bear wagged his tail but continued barking at the stairs. Toby tried to scuttle back into a corner but realized no spot was safe from the outside elements. Heidi walked down the steps and bent over to peek under the small landing.

"Oh, my goodness. It's the kitty from next door." Heidi stood and shook her finger at the excited dog. "Stop it, Bear. Let the kitty out."

Toby watched as Bear backed away from the steps.

"Sit, and stay, Bear," Heidi ordered.

Bear sat and stayed, but not still. Toby could see the fluffy white tail wagging excitedly. The next thing Toby saw was the little girl on her hands and knees, looking in at him, a big smile on the child's face. She was reaching for him.

"Careful, Alora," Hiedi called out. "We don't know if the kitty is friendly. And if he's scared, he could scratch you."

You got it, lady … but if you keep the mutt under control, I'll be out of your way in no time. Toby began to inch forward, making sure he was crawling in a direction away from the kid. Pausing at the edge of the protected area, Toby noted how far it was to the fence. *Wonder if I can make it before that dog decides to disobey Heidi.*

However, before Toby realized what was happening, Heidi reached down and scooped the yard intruder up into her arms. He decided not to fight it. *Better safe up here than down there where the mutt is, or having the kid maul me!*

"There, there, kitty ... let's get you safely back on your side of the fence." Heidi headed for the gate and gave Bear a hard look when he tried to wiggle closer.

Heidi stepped onto the sidewalk and was just about ready to put Toby down when Jack stepped out onto his front porch and glanced over to his new neighbour's house.

Oh, no ... Jack's going to think I'm in trouble. Well, I sort of was ... hope he's not mad ... especially with what he sees now ... Heidi casting me out of her yard. Toby struggled to get out of Heidi's arms.

Sensing the cat wanted down, Heidi set Toby on the sidewalk. She looked over to Jack and waved. "I found something of yours," she grinned.

Whoa, lady! I'm not something ... I'm Detective Toby!

Jack laughed as he came down the steps and walked toward Heidi and Toby. "You'll have to forgive Toby for his intrusion. He and Emma—the lady who lived here before you—were best friends, and Toby visited her all the time." Jack looked directly at Toby. "Still miss her, don't you, old man?"

"Well, he's no bother—really. It's just that Bear can be a little over-zealous, and even though he wouldn't hurt a cat, his idea of playing might not fit in with your cat's." Heidi paused and cleared her throat. "By the way, I'm sorry for the commotion this morning. Bear usually doesn't go out so early. I'll try to make sure it doesn't happen again, or, to be truthful here since I am dealing with an animal, I'll be more judicious. The last thing I want is trouble with a neighbour."

Jack ran a hand through his hair and smiled sheepishly. "Well, it was a bit annoying, I'll admit. But, I'm retired; I can always catch up on my sleep with an afternoon nap."

After a few moments of uncomfortable silence, Heidi turned back toward her gate, where both Bear and Alora were waiting impatiently for her return. "Well, guess I better get back to these two," she stated, "and get back to my unpacking. Like I said, I'll try not to have Bear disturb the neighbourhood too early in the morning." Heidi glanced down at Toby. "You're welcome to come over, kitty; however, I'd suggest you just come to the front door and meow. Alora would love to get to know you. Just this morning, she was saying how she wanted a kitty, so, with a little luck, you might just save me from having to get one of my own."

Toby flipped his tail and turned toward home. *You won't be seeing much of me, lady. No way I'm going to be a babysitter for your kid … no way I'm going to subject myself to being mauled by her. You aren't my Emma and that mutt of yours … well, at least I knew where I stood with Duke; we hated each other. I have no intention of being friends and playing with your mutt!* Toby avoided Jack, who was still on the front porch, heading instead to the back door where his private entrance was.

A few moments after Toby got into the house, Jack entered the kitchen. He poured a cup of coffee and made his way back to the living room, plunking down in his easy-chair. Toby, realizing there was not going to be any more kibbles dropped in his dish, followed Jack and took up his position on the back of the couch.

"Rough morning, eh, old man," Jack opened the conversation, a twinkle in his eyes as he looked at his companion.

Toby stared at Jack. *You have no idea. We need to stay away from this woman, Jack. My cat senses are telling me she has something to hide—something big.* Toby returned his attention to the street. He noticed a long, black limo drive slowly by, slowing down at the house next door before moving on.

6

Heidi decided to let Alora and Bear play a little longer in the yard. She felt she could get more things unpacked on her own. As she opened the first box, she leaned over it and began to cry. This was Heidi's third move since escaping from the hell Cain had restrained her in, and Heidi wondered if it was even worth the bother to unpack. He'd seemed able to find her, no matter where she went, no matter what she did to try and hide her identity. Her mind wandered back...

> Lorenzo had continued coming for her every morning, and as the days passed, he'd looked more and more troubled. Cain had made himself absent since the beating, but Heidi noticed him coming and going at all hours, along with several men in black limos.
>
> One morning, a week after the incident, Heidi decided to take the leap. After all, what was the worst that could happen? Another beating? As she and Lorenzo watched Alora play with Bear—Lorenzo always brought the puppy out for Alora whenever Cain wasn't around—Heidi plunged forward with her well-thought-out plan. At least, at that point, she thought it was a reasonable plan.
>
> "I need to get out of here, Lorenzo," she began hesitantly.

When Lorenzo didn't reply, or even look at her, Heidi wasn't sure if she should continue. Nevertheless, she felt she had no other option. Her voice was barely a whisper as she asked her question: "Will you help me?"

Lorenzo's continued silence frightened Heidi. Maybe he wasn't the man she'd thought him to be. Possibly his act of conscience over what he'd witnessed a week ago was just that—an act. Finally, he spoke: "You don't know what you're asking of me," he whispered gruffly. "Your husband is a powerful man and not one that anyone would dare to cross."

Heidi laid a hand on Lorenzo's arm. She felt the muscles beneath his sweater tense. "You say Cain is a powerful man, but what I see in you is a kind man. Why you are working for my husband, I don't know—other than the money is good. I get that, I guess. Maybe you're here to be our salvation—mine and that little girl over there who is playing with Bear. Think about her, Lorenzo. Please. Remember last week when you came in and caught Cain beating me. He meant the first blow for Alora—an innocent child. I need you to help me save her from her father."

Lorenzo had no idea how Cain and Heidi had met, what their history was before he'd come to work for her husband. "How did you not see Cain for what he is before you married him, Heidi?" he questioned.

Heidi hesitated, not sure exactly how much she should tell Lorenzo. Finally, with a heavy sigh, "When we were first together, I couldn't believe what an amazing man he was. We met in Cuba. I went there for a week to have some alone time after my grandmother passed, and Cain was there getting over a recent break-up: he was so kind, so caring. There wasn't anything he wouldn't do for me to make me feel better and put a smile on my face again.

"Upon our return to Canada, we discovered we didn't live too far from each other. Cain continued his attentiveness, and I continued to lean on him. I went back to work, and everyone was pleased to see how happy I was, and then one day, they all saw the reason for my happiness. Cain stopped by my office and asked me out for lunch, and right in front of all my colleagues, he got down on one knee and pulled a ring box out of his pocket! I was speechless. After I said yes to Cain, the entire office staff clapped and cheered. We were married within the month, and he took me for a honeymoon in Italy. I didn't think I could be happier."

"And never once during this time, did you ever have a clue about who he actually was?" Lorenzo asked as he lit a cigarette.

"Not once," Heidi replied. "Truthfully, there was the odd time I felt something was off with him, sort of a brooding look I'd notice, but when I asked him if something was wrong, he would shrug his shoulders, smile, and tell me it was nothing. Just a work thing that I needn't bother my pretty head over. So I left it alone.

"Life went on. Cain suggested we move here to the country. He wanted me to quit my job ... said there was no need for me to work. I hesitated at first because I enjoyed working, but Cain was so convincing, and he begged me. Cain told me he'd always dreamed of living in the country, and he'd found the perfect place. He convinced me it would be a great place to raise a family when we decided to start one. So, I quit my job, and we moved here."

"When was the first time he hit you?" Lorenzo tossed his cigarette onto the walkway and ground it out with his foot.

"Not until after Alora was born. Before that, he'd just started getting evasive and non-attentive. The man I married had disappeared, and this remote, non-caring person had taken over his body. The rest is history, Lorenzo. You see what is going on here; you saw what he did to me. I'm begging you to help me and my child get away from Cain."

Lorenzo didn't say anything. He looked at his watch and said it was time to go back to the house. He hadn't even said he would think about it, and Heidi had a sinking feeling in her gut that she was doomed. If Lorenzo ran to his boss and told him about this conversation—about her plea for help to get away from him—Cain's wrath would rain down on her like never before. He might even kill her. She'd thought he was going to kill her during that first severe beating. If it hadn't been for Lorenzo's timely entrance, she might not be here today, pleading for help.

The week following Heidi's plea for help went by without further conversation between her and Lorenzo. He'd closed off entirely. What little ground Heidi thought she'd made seemed to have sunk into an abyss. The week after that, a severe rainstorm pummelled the area, and Lorenzo didn't show up. Heidi did her best to keep occupied with Alora, but couldn't help thinking she'd made a colossal mistake by asking Lorenzo. Her only saving grace was that Cain, when he'd come home for a couple days, was in a good mood. Almost like the old Cain—the one she'd met in Cuba, the one she'd married.

Finally, the sun broke through, and Lorenzo showed up at the door. Alora raced out into the yard, calling for Bear. Lorenzo hurried to the steel building and let Bear out of his enclosure. While Alora and Bear played, Lorenzo walked over to a picnic table that was sitting under a large oak tree. He motioned for Heidi to join him. Heidi's blood was racing as she sat down.

"I've given your request some thought," Lorenzo began, "and I think I'm going to help you."

Heidi gasped in surprise. "Are you sure?" was all she could manage to say.

Lorenzo nodded. "Unless you've had a change of heart?" His eyebrows creased questioningly.

"No, no. I need to get out of here. Cain has been okay the last couple times he's been home, but he's a time bomb waiting to explode. I have to remove my daughter from his control because I know sooner or later, he's going to try and take her from me—just because he can, and he knows it will hurt me."

"I agree." Lorenzo paused and lit a cigarette, so Heidi took the opportunity to ask him a question.

"I need to know why you are going to do this for me."

Lorenzo leaned forward. "Look, I've seen a lot of things in this life. Good things. Bad things. The bad things I've seen have an extensive range of bad; however, when it comes to beating on a woman …

well, my dad never touched my mom like that. My parents raised me right—to respect the opposite sex. That is why I am going to help you. But you are going to have to give me some time to put together a plan of action."

"How long?" Heidi asked anxiously, wanting it to be the next day.

"I'll let you know. Until then, life goes on as it is. Don't give Cain any idea that something is going on. Be yourself; keep a low profile. Don't appear anxious over anything. Whatever you do, don't change anything in your personality." Lorenzo ground his cigarette out in the ashtray on the table. "Time to go back inside," he said, standing and walking over to where Alora was playing with Bear. "Have to put the puppy away now," he said, taking hold of Bear.

"I want to play more," Alora protested.

"Not today, kid. Go see your mom."

Alora stamped her foot angrily and folded her arms across her chest. Her lip protruded in an oversized pout. Heidi, noticing what was happening, quickly called Alora over to her.

A month passed, without any mention of escaping.

Heidi finished putting away the last box of goods in the kitchen before going out to the back yard to enjoy some time with her daughter.

7

Cain was furious when he'd come home and found Heidi, Alora, and even the dog were gone from the house. Two years had passed now. Two years with not a concrete sign of his wife and child—until now. One of his former employees, who'd only left his employ due to illness, called Cain and said he thought he'd seen Heidi in the city of Brantford when he was there for a doctor's appointment. The sighting had taken place at a gas station where they'd both been filling gas. Cain's informant had turned so Heidi wouldn't see his face, he'd told Cain. The man was shrewd, and Cain was sorry the man wasn't able to work any longer. He was a loyal man. He'd given Cain the licence plate of the car Heidi was driving.

"The bitch changed her name!" Cain laughed when he saw the police report giving him the name of the owner of the red Volkswagen Heidi was driving. "I suppose she thought I'd never find her if she did that. It's a small world, *Heidi*. But I know who you really are—Jennifer—my wife. And anyone who belongs to me doesn't leave me. You should have known better."

Cain paced in the kitchen, thinking about what he was going to do to Jennifer when he dragged her back home. He still wondered who had helped her and couldn't help thinking that it might have been Lorenzo because he was Jennifer's only contact outside of Cain. Then again, Lorenzo had up and quit a month before his wife escaped, so that ruled the man out. Or did it?

The escape was obviously orchestrated seamlessly for it to have worked. Cain stopped by the sink and looked out at the backyard. He wondered if Jennifer knew what he did in the steel building. He knew she wasn't a stupid woman, just too innocent for her own good. Cain smiled as he thought about how easily he had duped the naïve girl on the beach in Cuba.

For him, it had started as a game. A holiday fling that he would discard as soon as he left Cuba. However, Jennifer had been likeable, and she was fantastic in bed, giving equally under the covers. She was interesting to talk to, unlike some of the previous airheads he'd dated. Cain had found himself falling for Jennifer. It didn't disturb him until it was too late, and he'd found himself putting a ring on her finger.

At first, Cain remained attentive, but he soon became bored with domestic life. Besides, his business needed his attention. Cain didn't trust others to be in control. So, he'd started going on what he told Jennifer were business trips. She didn't mind; she was working. They were both busy. Jennifer had tried to figure out what he did, but he managed to evade the questions by telling her he was a salesman, and that was all she needed to know. Then Jennifer told him she was pregnant! That threw him for a loop. It was bad enough being tied down to a woman while on home soil—Cain had never been a one-woman man at any point in his life—it was another to have a kid.

Cain decided to move his burdens to the country and soon enough found the perfect location—to keep his wife in tow and to run his business. The property was a win/win. Jennifer began complaining about the isolation and told him she was sorry for quitting her job. He told her she wouldn't have been working after the kid was born anyway. And then had come the day Cain decided to teach Jennifer a lesson. After teaching her the lesson, he'd made her his prisoner entirely.

The new man, Pete, Cain hired to take Lorenzo's place, exited the steel building. He leaned against the wall and lit a cigarette. Cain hated smoking—anything—but most of his hired help partook in one habit or another. Cain studied the man. He was in his mid-thirties, lean, rugged looking. He'd been around the block a few times already but had always managed to evade the law. Lorenzo had sworn by the guy.

Once again, Cain got a strange feeling thinking about Lorenzo, and the relationship he may have built up with Jennifer. Cain had seen the look on Lorenzo's face the day his employee had walked into the kitchen—when Cain had lost control of his temper and was beating on his wife. However, despite misgivings, Cain hadn't had time to watch Lorenzo, and there was never another time that gave him reason or concern.

Glancing at his watch, Cain sighed. It was time to get to work. One of the most massive shipments he'd ever negotiated would be arriving at midnight, and Cain needed to make room for it in the warehouse. Jennifer could wait. He had a good man on her, and she would soon have her life torn apart!

8

Toby was bothered by the limo that had driven down the street, pausing at Heidi's house. *May as well call Emma's place Heidi's now ... my Emma is gone, and I don't think she's coming back ... at least not to live. Now, about that limo ... too early in the day for a party of any kind ... middle of the week, so that would rule out a wedding most likely ... so, what was it doing here? Who is this woman that someone who owned such an expensive vehicle would be interested her—in where she lives? I'll need to keep my eye on her and the kid. Especially if they're in some kind of danger ... seems like she could be, as much as she didn't really want Jack and me around.*

Jack walked into the living room. "You miss her, don't you, old man? I do too." Jack rubbed Toby under the chin. "We'll see Emma again ... I'm sure she'll come for a visit, and if she doesn't happen this way, we'll go to her. In the meantime, I think our new neighbour is going to be okay." Jack reached for his hat on the hook by the door. "I've got some shopping to do; do you want to come along for the ride?"

Toby looked away. He wanted to keep an eye out for that limo in case it drove by again.

Heidi had her back to the street when the long, black limo drove by. The driver had enough of a look at the trio in the backyard to confirm it was the house where Cain's wife was hiding out. He opened his Bluetooth with a voice command: "Call the boss."

After going through the process, Cain's phone started ringing.

"Cain, here," the tone was crisp—cold.

"Mitch, here," the driver returned. "Your package is confirmed at the location you gave me. What do you want me to do next?"

"Come back to the office," Cain replied. "I'll let you know when it's time." A pause. "Mitch, before you come back, could you swing by Sam's place and pick up his payment? He's overdue."

"What if he don't have the money, boss?" Mitch's knuckles ached from lack of use.

"Give him a warning." Cain hung up.

Mitch smiled. He'd worked for Cain for three years and was the number one driver in his boss' fleet. Mitch had grown up on the wrong side of the tracks, and he first met Cain in a bar. Mitch had been heavily involved in a bar fight at the time. After the fight was over, Cain approached him and asked Mitch if he knew how to drive. Mitch nodded, and Cain offered him a job. The rest was history.

When Mitch walked into Sam's restaurant, it was the middle of the afternoon, so Mitch didn't expect a lot of clients to be around. There was a card league playing in one of the rooms; he'd have to be quiet with what he was about to do. Mitch walked up to the bar. "Sam in?" he asked the bartender.

The bartender jerked a thumb toward a door behind the bar. "In the office."

Mitch didn't bother to knock on the door. "Sam … Sam, my man," he mocked the man behind the big oak desk.

Sam's face blanched. "Mitch. Good to see you. Been a while." Sam's voice sounded strained.

"Really, Sam?" Mitch perched himself on the edge of the desk and picked a letter opener off of a pile of envelopes and balanced it on his pointer finger. "Behind in opening your mail, Sam?"

Sam swallowed hard, his Adam's apple bobbing in his throat. "A bit," he mumbled.

"Well, Sam, it's like this. It was conveyed to my attention that you're behind in something else, too. So, Cain sent me here to encourage you to pay what you owe." Mitch stabbed the letter opener into the pile of envelopes, and it wobbled a couple of seconds before falling over. "Do you have what's owing so I can leave and you can get on with your day?"

Sam reached his hand toward the top drawer of his desk.

"You better not be reaching for a gun," Mitch warned. "It won't end well for you."

"My chequebook's in here," Sam stuttered.

Mitch burst out laughing. "Do you think Cain will be pleased with me if I take him a rubber cheque from you? Come on, man, you know better than that! Cain only deals in cash." Mitch jumped off the desk. He reached over, pulled up a pant leg, and took out a knife. "I don't want to hurt you, Sam, truthfully, I don't. So, how say you just open your safe there and get me the money."

"I don't have it." Sam looked away from Mitch's hard stare.

Mitch sauntered up behind Sam. and ran the tip of the knife along Sam's chin line, pressing harder as he neared the end of the chin bone. "What do you suggest I do now? I can't go back to Cain empty-handed." Mitch didn't give Sam time to answer the question: "Tell you what, I'll sleep on it tonight and I'll come back in the morning to collect—one thing or another." Mitch lowered the knife and slapped Sam's cheek. With that, Mitch took his leave.

On the way out of the bar, Mitch told the bartender that his boss might need a stiff drink. Inside the office that Mitch had just left, Sam pounded a fist on his desk before picking up his phone to make a call.

Mitch decided to drive by the house where he'd seen Heidi before checking into a hotel for the night. All was quiet on the street. No lights were on in the homes.

However, two sets of eyes were watching him. Toby didn't like the fact that the black limo slowed down again as it drove past, leaving him to believe that he'd been right. Heidi was in some kind of trouble.

Bear growled as he recognized a car he'd seen a hundred times on the farm!

9

Toby was bothered by the limo that had driven by, and though he tried to sleep, he couldn't. Dreams inundated his mind. His inner fears manifested themselves in bold images of a man getting out of the car and taking the little girl out of the backyard. Alora was struggling, and as she tried to scream, an enormous hand clapped over her mouth. The man threw the kid into the backseat of the limo, looked around, then joined her in the vehicle. He was faceless—just a hulking body. Someone else drove the limo, but Toby couldn't see them due to the blacked-out windows. As the dream continued, making its way back to the yard next door, the dog showed up, laying as though asleep while its little charge was taken.

The next dream wasn't any better. In this one, Heidi lay on her kitchen floor, blood trickling from a wound on her head. Toby startled awake, not able to take any more of the horror he saw in the dream world. He sat up unsteadily, and looked out at the early morning.

Something is terribly wrong next door … I am sure of this now. I guess I'll have no alternative but to infiltrate my detective skills into Hiedi's life. Not that I like kids … or dogs … but that man, despite being faceless, didn't seem like he had any good intentions towards my new neighbours. I hope whatever they did to the dog, it's not dead. I mean, dogs are my prime enemies—after criminals, of course—but I don't want to see the furry white thing dead! It was just a dream … maybe I'm reading too much into it. Then again, perhaps I'm not.

Toby stretched and made his way off the couch and into the kitchen. He could hear Jack rustling around in the bathroom down the hallway and knew breakfast would be served in short order.

Heidi's sleep had been restless. When she woke in the morning, she had an inkling that something was wrong. Heidi faintly recalled hearing Bear growling downstairs, unusual for him unless there was something wrong. But she'd been tired and hadn't bothered to check out what was going on. Heidi walked down the hallway to the bathroom, passing by Alora's room. She looked in and stared at her daughter for a few moments—her beautiful daughter.

Alora was sleeping peacefully. Her dark curls cascaded over the pillow; her face was rosy and free of worry. One of her feet stuck out from under the covers. Heidi smiled, then continued on her way. She'd do anything to protect Alora, but would all that she'd done be enough to keep Cain away? Cain and his thugs!

Heidi leaned over the sink and stared into the mirror. She noticed the wrinkles beginning to creep onto the landscape of her skin, and felt she was much too young to have so many. Dark circles fought to take over the area around Heidi's eyes—a sign of lack of sleep, or was it from worrying who might be around the next corner? Heidi turned on the tap and splashed some water on her face. She'd skip her shower for this morning because she was just going to get sweaty anyway as she finished the unpacking.

As Heidi walked back past Alora's room, she heard her little girl stirring. From downstairs, Bear was whining, wanting outside. Heidi checked her watch. It was time. She hoped he'd be able to keep his barking at bay so as not to wake up the entire neighbourhood. Heidi popped her head into Alora's room: "Awake, sweet pea? Mommy has to go downstairs and let Bear out. Get dressed and come down for breakfast; what would you like this morning?"

"You said we could have pancakes and sausage this morning," Alora giggled with a little-girl stern look on her face.

Heidi laughed. "That I did. Well, I haven't gotten groceries yet, so I don't think we have any sausages. The pancake mix is accessible, though. How say we just do them for breakfast and then go to the store later and pick up some sausages for supper?" Heidi hoped her proposal would satisfy Alora.

Alora heaved a big sigh and smirked. "Okay, Mommy," she replied, getting out of her bed and rushing toward the door. "Gotta go pee," she said on the run to the bathroom.

"See you downstairs soon," Heidi commented, heading to the stairway.

Bear started jumping up and down at the back door as soon as he heard the footsteps approaching. Heidi opened the doors for her faithful companion and Bear bound out into the yard. Right away, he started barking and chasing a squirrel. "Bear!" Heidi shouted, "Quiet!" Bear looked back at his mistress and wagged his tail, then went quietly about the business he was supposed to.

Heidi returned to the house, hoping Bear wouldn't start barking again. As she entered the kitchen, Alora was just coming downstairs, still in her pyjamas.

"Pancakes ready yet?" Alora asked.

"I'm not superwoman," Heidi chuckled, heading to the cupboard and pulling out the box of pancake mix. "Get Mommy a mixing bowl from the counter over there, please," Heidi said, pointing to a pile of bowls she hadn't gotten around to putting away yet.

The kitchen soon filled with the savoury smell of maple pancakes. Before sitting down to their breakfast, Heidi let Bear in the house and filled his dish with kibble. Everything was peaceful at that moment. Heidi looked at her two charges and prayed it remained so. Lorenzo had been nervous the last time they'd met, before making the third move in two years. He told her that his inside contact informed him that Cain was becoming more obsessed with finding her. Heidi knew who Lorenzo's inside man was; he'd been the one to get her, Alora, and Bear out of the house, taking them to the drop zone where Lorenzo had taken over. Heidi said a little prayer for Pete, as well.

Toby decided to walk over to Heidi's and check out the landscape. He'd noticed Bear had been out for an early-morning romp but had been hushed by Heidi after a couple of minutes of barking. Instead of going under the fence as he'd done when Emma had lived next door, Toby took Heidi's advice and made his way to the front door. He jumped on to the windowsill and meowed loudly. Within seconds, Bear raced into the living room and started barking at the door.

"Bear!" Heidi followed close on his heels, and Toby could tell she was about to say something more, but she noticed Toby at the window and went straight to the door, pushing Bear aside. She cracked the door. "What can I do for you, Toby?" she asked as though the cat could understand what she was saying.

Toby rushed to the opening, meowed, and circled around.

Alora was standing behind her mom, and her face lit up at the sight of Toby. "Can you let the kitty in? Please, Mommy." Alora pulled on her mother's arm.

Toby wasn't sure what he had hoped to accomplish by coming over. Not to come face to face with the dog, that was for sure. Heidi noticed Toby's hesitation, and also that Bear was trying to push his way out to get to their visitor. "Just a moment, Toby … I'll put Bear outside and let you in. Once Bear settles down, I'll formally introduce you two." Heidi shut the door, and Toby jumped back up onto the window sill and watched as Heidi took Bear by the collar and led him to the back door. Within a few seconds, she returned to the front door and let Toby into the house.

Immediately, Alora accosted him. "Nice kitty," she exclaimed, kneeling and reaching out to pet Toby. Toby almost cringed away, but then he remembered why he was there—to check things out. He allowed the kid to hug him.

"Not too tight now, Alora. You don't want to hurt the kitty." Heidi smiled. "Why don't you play with Toby while I finish emptying the boxes in the kitchen?"

Really! Leave me in here with the kid! No way, lady. Toby wiggled out of Alora's grasp and followed Heidi to the kitchen. He shuddered as he remembered the last time he'd been in this room—right after seeing what Emma had been up to in the basement. *I wonder how Mike is doing, and if Janine went back to him … everything here looks normal now, though … what the hell are you doing here, Toby?* Toby wandered around the kitchen, narrowly avoiding Alora several times as she continued to attempt to play with him. Finally, she gave up and asked her mom if she could go outside and play with Bear. Heidi nodded approval.

Toby stayed around, watching Heidi for another half an hour. He couldn't see anything amiss and began thinking he was making too much out of the limo. He decided to head home, so he went to the front door, sat down, and meowed to be let out. Heidi walked up to him, but instead of opening the door, she knelt beside him: "How about I take you out in the backyard, and you and Bear get acquainted."

Before Toby could protest, Heidi scooped him up in her arms and walked towards the back door. Stepping out into the yard, she called Bear over. Toby struggled to get free, but Heidi held him secure. As Bear got closer, Heidi raised a hand for him to slow down, and then told him to sit. Once the dog was sitting, Heidi scratched Toby behind the ears and set him down on the grass.

"Bear won't move now, Toby, so check him out. If we are going to be neighbours, I think you two should get to know each other and become friends."

As Toby circled Bear, he happened to glance at the street. There was the limo again, driving slowly by the house. Suddenly, Bear let out a growl. Toby observed that Bear was looking in the same direction as he was. *Maybe we can be friends after all!*

10

Mitch couldn't help himself. Despite his dedication to his boss, he couldn't help himself when he saw a beautiful woman. And Jennifer was a beautiful woman! Obviously, she had no use for Cain or she would have stayed with him. Mitch began to formulate a plan of how he could meet Jennifer and seduce her. He'd have to get rid of the kid first, though For now, he had to deal with a man named Sam.

Mitch pressed his foot on the gas and moved on down the road. Five minutes later, Mitch pulled up to Sam's place and shut the engine off. He took out his phone and made a call to Cain.

"Cain here."

"Mitch. Thought I'd fill you in on Sam; as of yesterday, Sam didn't have the money…"

"Did you ask him if he still has the goods?" Cain inquired. Mitch detected a hint of annoyance in his boss' tone.

"No. I guess I didn't think about that. Gave Sam a suitable warning that he better have the money today. I'm sitting outside his place right now. How far do you want me to go?" Mitch asked, despite knowing that when you worked for Cain, and someone crossed him, it didn't matter what lines you crossed.

The answer Mitch expected was forthcoming. "Why are you even asking me, Mitch? Get the job done and bring me my money—or the goods if there are any left." The line closed.

Mitch clicked his phone off and chuckled. This was one part of the job he loved. Mitch got out of the car and went around to the trunk. Inside, under where a spare tire was, Mitch lifted out a leather case and opened it. He ran his fingers lovingly over the cold, steel barrel of the gun and sighed. Then, he screwed on the silencer and stuck the gun in his belt on his left side. Closing the trunk, Mitch sauntered to the front door.

The breakfast crowd was sparse, and only one waitress was serving the four tables. Mitch glanced at the bar, but of course, the bartender wouldn't be working yet. Not until noon.

"Have a seat, sir; I'll be with you in a moment," the waitress called back as she went to the kitchen to pick up an order.

Mitch didn't bother to reply. There was no need. He made his way to the bar and stepped behind it to the office door. There was also no need to knock. Inside the office, Mitch saw Sam standing by the window, staring out into the morning.

"Morning, Sam," Mitch greeted.

Silence.

Mitch didn't waste any time getting to the point. "Do you have what I came for?"

Slowly, Sam turned to face the intruder. "I have some," he finally managed to croak out.

"Do you still have some of the goods?"

Sam shook his head.

Mitch perched himself on the edge of the desk. He picked up the letter opener, as he had done the night before, but this time he tapped it on his palm. "So," Mitch began, "let me get this straight … just so there isn't any misunderstanding between us. You sold all the goods, got paid, and spent the money … on what?"

"I didn't get paid for some of it," Sam looked down at the floor. Mitch noticed the man's hands shaking.

Mitch set the letter opener back on the desk. "I see. So, what you're saying is that you have the same problem I do. Someone isn't paying their debt." Mitch jumped off the desk and walked over to the window, getting up close and personal to Sam. "What do you do when someone doesn't pay you, Sam?"

Sam cleared his throat a couple of times before answering. "I … I … I just keep on them until they pay up," Sam stuttered, avoiding looking at Mitch.

"Really?" Mitch's tone was harsh. "Do you realize who you're lying to, Sam? I know all about you and what you do to people who don't pay their debts to you. I've had to clean up a couple of your messes in the past. Is there a mess you need me to handle for you, Sam?"

Sam shook his head.

"Well, let's make a deal then. Give me what you have of the hundred thousand, and for every thousand you're short, I'll take off one of your fingers. And if they aren't enough, I'll start with your toes. How does that sound?" Mitch smirked.

Sam seemed to gain a speck of courage, false as it was. He straightened his shoulders and looked Mitch in the eyes. "No need to go that far. I'll give you what I have, and if you give me till the end of today, I'll have the rest. I just couldn't reach the guy last night. His wife said he was out of town and would be back today after lunch."

"Is that how you'd handle such a situation, Sam … give your man more time?"

"Yeah … yeah, that's how I'd handle it."

"What if your guy doesn't have your money? What do we do then? Maybe kidnap his wife … if he has kids, we could take them. Surely he'd come up with the money then. What do you think, Sam? Do you need help with any of this?"

"No. I'll handle it."

Mitch made to turn away, then stopped. He lifted a finger in the air. "You know, Sam, there's one thing bothering me." Mitch paused for effect, watching Sam closely, noticing the man's skin pale. "Why is it you didn't call Cain and tell him you were having trouble collecting? Cain was nice enough to extend you the credit until you got paid since it was such a large amount … but for you to ignore your debt…" Another break. "Do you want to know what I think, Sam?" Without waiting for an answer, Mitch continued. "I think you were thinking you could get away without paying your debt. I believe you pocketed the money … maybe you were thinking of getting out of town … perhaps you thought Cain wouldn't care about a few thousand dollars … after all, Cain is a wealthy man … but you know all this, don't you?"

"You've got it all wrong…" Sam began, but Mitch cut him off.

"I'll tell you what we're going to do here," Mitch began. "You're going to go over to your safe and give me all the money you have in there. And then, you're going to write down the name of the man who owes you money so I can do your job for you."

Sam didn't like the route the conversation was taking. He knew how ruthless Cain's thug, Mitch, could be. Despite his customer not paying him, Sam didn't want anything to happen to the man's family. They were innocent in all this. "I told you, I'd handle it. I'll have your money by the end of the day, even if I have to go to the bank and take out a loan," Sam finished, hoping that would satisfy the madman in front of him.

Mitch, as though he hadn't heard a word Sam had said, walked over to the safe. He pulled the gun out of his belt and tapped it on the metal door. "No, Sam. I think we'll do this my way. Open the safe. Now!"

Sam, realizing he wasn't going to have a choice in the matter, resigned himself to the situation. He started towards the safe and knelt to open the door, his hand shaking as he whirled the dial around. He reached inside and took out a stack of hundred dollar bills.

"All of it," Mitch said, putting the gun muzzle to Sam's temple.

Sam reached inside the safe and took out the rest of the money. He stood and walked to the desk, piling the four stacks of bills on the corner.

"Good man, Sam." Mitch followed Sam to the desk; his gun pointed at the nervous man. "Now, the name and I'll get out of your hair, and you can get on with your day."

Sam picked up a pen, shuffled around for a blank paper, and wrote down the requested name.

"Address, too."

Sam obliged. As he handed the slip of paper to Mitch, "Please don't hurt the wife and kids. Can you at least promise me that?" he begged.

Mitch smirked and tucked the name and address into his pocket. "Sorry, Sam. I can't make a promise I have no intention of keeping."

A few moments later, Mitch left the restaurant. Sam would never take advantage of Cain again. Before putting his car into drive, Mitch punched the address of his next stop into the GPS. When Cameron arrived home this afternoon, he'd pay what was owing without hesitation!

11

Toby looked back at Heidi to see if she'd noticed the limo, as well. She had. Her face had blanched, and her hands had begun shaking. *I was right. Heidi and the kid are in some sort of trouble. Boy, do I have a nose for sniffing out damsels in distress.* Toby walked over to Heidi, totally oblivious to the dog, and rubbed around her legs. To his surprise, Bear went to his mistress and settled at her feet, moaning. *All I have to do now is get Jack to realize our neighbour is in trouble and get him to investigate to find out what that trouble is!*

Deciding he'd had enough for one morning, Toby looked up at Heidi and meowed, then proceeded to his escape route in the fence. He knew there wasn't going to be any issues with Bear; he was a friendly dog and wouldn't do any harm. As he wiggled under the fence, he heard Alora saying goodbye to him.

Jack was on the phone with his girlfriend, Tessa, when Toby got home. It was good to see Jack relaxed, but if the neighbour was in the trouble Toby thought she was in, Jack's downtime was going to be short-lived. Jack glanced briefly at Toby, who had jumped up on the couch beside him, rotating around before climbing onto Jack's lap.

"Hang on a minute, Tessa," Jack laughed. "It appears Toby is trying to tell me something … what's up, old man?"

Toby jumped down and went to the front door, sat, and meowed loudly. He scratched at the door.

"Well, I guess I better leave off this conversation," Jack said into the receiver. "I'll see you tonight for supper." Jack hung up the phone and turned his attention to Toby. "What do you want, old man … for me to follow you somewhere?"

Toby circled and scratched at the door again. *If I can just get Jack over there, maybe he'll take the hint and invite Heidi for supper—a welcome to the neighbourhood gesture.* To Toby's surprise, Jack figured out what he wanted.

"I think I know what it is, old man … you've spent the last couple of hours next door, and you believe our new neighbours aren't so bad after all, and you want me to invite them for supper. Is that it, old man?"

Toby meowed softly, and rubbed around Jack's legs, then proceeded to the kitchen, confirming Jack's assumption. Jack slipped out the front door and made his way to Heidi's. She was still in the back yard, cleaning out weeds from the flower garden. "Hello there," Jack called out. "Looks like you're working hard," he added. *How lame are you, of course, she's working hard!*

Heidi looked up. "Yeah, thought I'd get some of these weeds out of here while the weather is still half-decent. What can I do for you … Jack, wasn't it?"

"Yeah, Jack … Since you're working so hard there, and have just moved in, I reckon you need a good home-cooked meal for you and the little one. My girlfriend is coming over for supper tonight, and I'd like to invite you and your daughter to join us."

Heidi stood and strolled over to the fence where Jack was standing. She studied him on her way, debating if she should get involved with the neighbour. Seeing the limo earlier had shaken her up. On the other hand, Jack was a retired cop, and she just might need someone like that on her side. "What time?" she asked, leaning on the fence.

"What's best for you … 5:30 or 6?

"Let's do 6." Before turning away, Heidi said, "Thank you."

Jack watched Heidi return to her gardening. "I think I've been hanging around Toby too long. Something's going on with this young woman. I can tell from her carriage." Jack made his way home to give Toby the good news.

12

Mitch pulled up across the street from the address Sam had given him. He noticed two children playing in the front yard, a boy and a girl. He saw the living room curtain open; a woman looked out, knocked on the window, smiled, and waved to the children. "She's a looker," Mitch said to the empty car. "Maybe, after I finish with her husband, I'll get a piece of her!"

There was still about an hour before Cameron was due home. Mitch could learn a lot during that hour. The comings and goings in the neighbourhood. Those kinds of details were necessary for what he might have to do. Hopefully not. Even Mitch had a conscience, and he'd not like to see two children grow up without a father—as he had.

Mitch thought back to his childhood before his father left the family, and then his teen years afterward. He'd lived in fear of his father when he was little: fear of the beatings he'd receive for no apparent reasons; fear of the beatings his mother would take to protect him—when she was able. Mitch's father was a salesman who worked long hours, sometimes gone for a week at a time. When he came home from those trips, he was always miserable.

As Mitch got older, his temper increased, and he swore he'd never let his father hit him again, or his mother. But he'd never been strong enough to fight the big man who walked through their door. Mitch never got the chance to fight back. After his father left for good, when Mitch was thirteen, Mitch began to work out in earnest at the local gym.

His father had left Mitch's mom bleeding on the floor before walking out on the family, and his mother had never walked again, the damage was so severe. She was the one soft-spot in Mitch's heart—the only vulnerability he had. Currently, his mother was in a nursing home, and he paid for the best care possible for her.

A car approached and started to slow down as it drew closer to where Mitch was parked. Woman driver, Mitch noticed. Not Cameron. He closed his eyes, pretending he was asleep. The car moved on, and when Mitch opened his eyes, he saw the vehicle pull into a driveway a couple doors down from Cameron's house.

Mitch sat up in his seat when he saw the front door of Cameron's house open. Cameron's wife stepped out onto the porch and called the children inside. The girl obeyed immediately; the boy dragged his feet. Once the trio was inside, Mitch turned the key in the ignition and pulled away from the curb. He'd park the vehicle one street over by a park he'd noticed, then return through the unfenced backyards he'd seen. It was time to visit Cameron's family.

When the front door opened to Mitch's ring, a boy of around ten confronted him. *A third kid! This isn't going to be easy. Key will be to frighten them all enough … have to get to mommy dearest first.* "Is your mother home, son?" Mitch asked nonchalantly.

The kid turned and hollered: "Carrie! Someone for you at the door."

Mitch heard footsteps approaching, and within seconds, a young woman appeared around the corner. Mitch hoped it was the wife. For all he knew, it could be a babysitter: after all, the kid had called the woman by her first name. He took a plunge, hoping this was going to go down as planned.

"Sorry to bother you, ma'am. I'm a friend of your husband and just happened to be in town on business. Is Cameron home?" Mitch noticed the two children he'd seen in the yard, standing in the hallway. The boy who'd answered the door slunk off.

The woman studied Mitch for a moment before answering. Even then, her words came out hesitantly. "Ah ... Cameron isn't here right now, and, ah, he didn't mention he was expecting a visitor..."

"Oh, excuse me, ma'am ... thought I'd surprise Cam—I haven't seen him for years. We went to school together..."

"Oh, which school?" the woman asked suspiciously.

Damn! "BCI," Mitch replied, taking a shot that would be the high school Cameron had attended. "I was only there for my senior year, but Cam and I hit it off pretty quickly. I thought I'd look him up while I'm in town."

The woman's eyes still told Mitch that she wasn't sure about the man standing on her step. Mitch was getting impatient. The longer he stood in the open, the better chance someone might see him, which would make the situation more difficult to pull off. Finally, the woman opened the door wider and motioned for Mitch to come in.

"I guess you can wait in the living room for Cameron," she pointed to a room to the left of the entrance. "Would you like a coffee?" she asked, shutting the front door and clicking the lock into place.

"Very kind of you to ask," Mitch replied, "but no thanks."

"Okay, then. Just make yourself at home. Cameron will be here soon. I have to finish the supper prep." The woman disappeared down the hallway.

Mitch felt someone was watching him, and when he turned toward the living room entrance, he saw the two kids from the yard standing in the doorway, staring at him. He thought his best move was to be friendly. If he could manipulate these two to get closer, he'd get them tied up. The woman would be easy as a piece of cake to control after that.

"Who are you?" the boy asked. He looked to be around seven.

Mitch smiled. "A friend of your dad." Mitch pointed to some pictures on the wall. "Are these pictures of your family?" he asked.

The children stepped into the room, and the little girl pointed to the picture of her. "That's me," she said excitedly.

"You're a little cutie, aren't you," Mitch commented. "And this must be you." Mitch pointed to another picture and directed his question to the boy.

"Yeah, that's when I was five. Mommy hasn't put my new picture up yet," the boy replied.

"Who's this?" Mitch pointed to the third picture of a sullen-looking boy, much resembling the child who'd opened the door. He didn't look like the other two kids.

"Our step-brother," the boy replied. Then, remembering to give his name, "Colin … he's not very nice to us."

Mitch grinned. *That explains things then.* Mitch noticed a photo album on the coffee table and picked it up. Sitting on the couch, he patted the cushion beside him. "Want to show me the pictures and tell me who everyone is? I haven't seen your dad for a few years, and it would be good to catch up on what he's been doing with his life." The little girl jumped on the couch right away; the boy followed after a moment.

"What's your name?" the boy asked.

"Mitch. What's yours?"

"Devlin."

"What about your name, little lady?" Mitch was trying hard to sound nice.

"Cindy," the little girl giggled.

For the next few minutes, Mitch looked through the album and listened to the children as they talked about the pictures. He learned a lot about Cameron's family, and it was with a hint of trepidation that he finally had to make his move. Mitch needed to ensure that Cameron would have no choice but to play ball when he got home and found his family in danger.

Having secured the two children with ties and Duct tape over their mouths, Mitch left the living room and sauntered to the kitchen where he knew Cameron's wife would be. Mitch had no idea where the stepson was.

"Did you change your mind about a coffee?" the woman asked when she saw Mitch approaching. "I hope the children didn't bother you too much; I heard them chatting your ears off," she added.

Mitch smiled. Had Cameron's wife been looking closely at the man in her kitchen, she would have noticed that his eyes were not smiling. They were cold. "Actually, your little girl, Cindy, spilled something on the carpet, and I just came to get a cloth to clean it up," Mitch said.

Cameron's wife threw the spoon she'd used to stir the spaghetti sauce into the sink. She grabbed some paper towels and raced to the living room.

Easy-peasy… Cameron followed her, and soon she joined her two children, shock on her face. "Just in time for the show," Mitch said as he heard a car pull into the driveway. "It'll be over soon, though, Carrie, as long as Cameron cooperates."

Carrie struggled against the restraints. Her eyes were wide with fear, and something else, Mitch noticed—hatred. Mitch wondered how much she knew about her husband's business dealings. Mitch moved to the window and cracked the curtain so he could watch Cameron walk toward the house. A noise in the hallway caused Mitch to turn. He'd forgotten about the stepson.

"Carrie! Where are you?" the kid called out.

Mitch moved quickly to the doorway of the living room and caught the boy just before he reached his destination. The ten-year-old was a little more difficult to subdue than the younger children had been, and Mitch had to use extra force to contain the boy. He carried the limp body into the living room and bound his hands, then taped the boy's mouth. Just in time, too.

13

Cameron stepped into the house and called out for his wife. When she didn't answer, he called again. "Carrie! I'm home, honey. Kids! Where's your mom?" Cameron asked, walking toward the kitchen.

Mitch looked at his four prisoners, stashed behind the couch, out of sight of anyone who might pass by the living room. He smiled at the group. Carrie struggled against her restraints again, and Mitch could see her throat muscles contracting as she tried to scream. Tears streaked down Cindy's and Devlin's faces. The older boy hadn't come to yet. Mitch meandered out to the kitchen.

Cameron heard the footsteps approaching him. He turned: "Carrie?" His face turned white when he saw it wasn't his wife.

"Carrie's a bit tied up at the moment," Mitch smirked. He moved his hand to the gun he'd secured in his belt. "Along with the children," he added.

"Who are you, and what do you want?" Cameron demanded angrily, although there was a hint of fear trickling through his words.

"I think we have a mutual friend … *had* a mutual friend. Sam." Mitch waited for a reaction.

Cameron tilted his head to the side, as though he didn't know who Mitch was talking about.

"Don't play dumb with me, Cameron. Sam, before he expired, gave me your name and address. How does it feel to be responsible for someone's death, Cameron? You owed Sam a lot of money, which, he, in turn, owed to my boss for the goods Sam bought from him and sold to you."

Cameron tried to gather his thoughts, attempting to figure a way out of the predicament he'd put himself and his family in. He'd sold the goods and invested the money off-shore instead of paying Sam.

Mitch continued. "My boss wants his money, and he's not a patient man. Neither am I. So, if you just want to get the money for me now, I'll leave, and there's no harm done."

Cameron wanted to buy some time before he told the intruder that there was no money to be had—not immediately, anyway. Finally, "I don't have it here in the house. You'll have to give me a couple of days to access it."

"You have to be kidding me, Cameron!" Mitch snorted. "Do you know what I think? I think you spent the money. I think it was very unwise of you. Have I hit the nail on the head, Cameron?"

Cameron's mind was spinning with what scenario he was going to tell this man to save his life and that of his family. "I didn't spend the money," Cameron began. "I secured it in an account until I sold all the goods. I've been having a difficult time moving some of it. A lot of competition on the street."

"Why is it that I don't believe you?" Mitch took the gun out of his belt and swung it around, then pointed it directly at Cameron. "Get me the money or the goods. Now! Only option you have here, Cameron." Mitch made his move toward Cameron, holding the gun against his back. "Let's take a little walk down the hallway to the living room where you can see your family."

The fight was going out of Cameron. He knew he'd screwed up royally this time. He hadn't told Carrie of his layoff. He hadn't told her about his meeting with Sam and what he'd done to try and raise enough money so they could get out of the city. He'd just come home from talking to a real estate agent and had signed papers to put the house on the market. Cameron figured with the money he realized from the house, and the money he—and his family—had stashed overseas, he could make a clean getaway. The realtor had told him that she had someone whom she thought would be quite interested in buying a house in Cameron's neighbourhood. Cameron staggered as Mitch gave him a shove.

When the two men entered the living room, Cameron collapsed to the carpet and began to cry. "Please, mister, whoever you are … don't hurt my family. Take me … do what you want with me, but don't hurt them. They don't know anything about what I've done."

Mitch wasn't in the mood to kill children. He thought of another way to get what he needed. He pulled Cameron to his feet and shoved him onto the couch. "Tell you what, Cameron. You tell this little wife of yours that you are going to go with me and that if she even breathes a word to anyone about what has happened here—her or one of the children—it will be the last time she sees you. Alive. Once I have what I came for, I'll let you go, and I know you wouldn't want the police to become aware of what you've been doing on the side, would you, Cameron?"

Cameron shook his head.

"So, why don't you tell Carrie what you've been up to so she will understand the importance of keeping her mouth shut, and ensure the kids don't tell anyone, either," Mitch suggested. "Go ahead, Cameron. Be a man and fess up to the little woman."

Cameron straightened up on the couch, stood, and turned to face his wife. The first words out of his mouth were an apology. "I'm so sorry, Carrie. I never meant for any of this to happen." Cameron swallowed hard, his Adam's apple bobbing nervously. "I lost my job a couple of months ago, and instead of telling you, I thought I could do something else that would get us out of debt. I got involved with some nasty people. I didn't know at the time just how bad they were. Instead of paying my debt to them, I put the money somewhere else. I just signed papers to sell our house, and once it sold, I was going to move us out of this city."

Mitch was watching Carrie's face and could tell she wasn't pleased with what her husband was confessing. Mitch decided to take the tape from her mouth and let her question Cameron—give him shit for the predicament he'd put his family in. Mitch assisted Carrie to her feet. As soon as the tape was off, she turned on her husband with an outrage worthy of an academy award.

"How dare you, Cameron! How dare you put your children and me into such danger! What were you thinking? And now, you expect me to protect you..."

"Our children, Carrie ... we have to do this to protect them," Cameron stammered.

"Oh, was it them you were thinking of when you went off and got involved with those nasty people?—When you decided to do something illegal? I don't think so." Carrie turned to Mitch. "You can have him, mister ... whoever you are. Just take him and leave. I won't say a word to anyone."

"Carrie..." Cameron started to plead.

"Don't Carrie me, Cameron. We're done!" Carrie looked at Mitch. "Take him. You have my word; I won't breathe a word to anyone."

Mitch studied the woman in front of him and wondered if she was telling the truth. He was good at reading people, but was she better at charades. Was she just saying all this to her husband so she could get away with her kids? Maybe she knew about the money, where it was, and how to get to it. Mitch looked from her to the children, then back to Cameron.

"What do you think, Cameron," Mitch pointed the gun at Carrie. "Is your wife telling the truth, or is she your partner in crime?"

"I'm not his partner in anything anymore!" Carrie hissed.

Mitch lowered the gun and pointed it toward Cameron. "You heard the lady; I guess she doesn't want anything more to do with you." Looking back at Carrie, "Make sure you are true to your word or I'll be back, and next time I won't be so pleasant, and definitely not so forgiving. You wouldn't want anything to happen to your children now, would you? I hope you understand me, Carrie?"

Carrie nodded.

Mitch waved the gun at Cameron. "Get up. We're going out the back door. My vehicle is by the park, a street over from here. Don't even think of making a move. And to ensure you don't, let's take … hmm, which kid shall we take with us … the boy, Devlin."

"I thought you were going to leave us alone," Carrie cried out, struggling against her restraints.

"Oh, I won't hurt him," Mitch stated. "He's just my insurance to get your husband away from here. The boy will return from the park after we're gone and he'll be able to untie all of you. How does that sound?"

Carrie's shoulders slumped in defeat. Mitch noticed her movement, and, once again, had the feeling she was playing a game. However, there wasn't time to debate anything now. Mitch pulled Devlin to his feet and pulled the tape from his mouth. Devlin winced in pain, but no other sound was forthcoming. Fear seized hold of the kid.

"You heard the plan, boy?" Mitch asked.

Devlin nodded.

"Okay, then. Let's get moving."

14

Heidi took a quick shower after finishing in the garden. She dressed conservatively, blue jeans and a pale-blue sweater, then went downstairs to the living room where Alora was watching television.

"Would you like me to braid your hair?" Heidi asked Alora.

"Yes, please, Mommy."

"One or two?"

"One."

"Okay, run and get your brush and an elastic."

As Heidi ran the brush through Alora's hair, then began the braid, "Are you happy here?" she asked as she placed the elastic on the end of the braid.

"Oh, yes, Mommy. I like our new neighbours, especially Toby." Alora's eyes lit up with excitement.

"So, you'd be unhappy if we had to move from here?" Heidi sighed. Having seen the black limo, a familiar sight from the country house, she couldn't get out of her head that Cain had found her. There was no way she'd go back to him. No way she would subject Alora to his world. Then again, maybe it was just any limo. After all, lots of people could own one.

"Are you okay, Mommy?" Alora cut into her mother's thoughts.

Heidi pulled Alora to her for a hug. "I'm fine, sweetheart. Let's go and have supper with Jack and Toby."

Toby was watching out his window for Heidi and Alora. He hoped they'd leave the dog home and smiled a cattish grin when he saw only two humans walking toward the house. No dog. Good. Toby raced to the front door and meowed.

"Are they here?" Jack said, coming into the living room, wiping his hands on a towel. He threw the towel over his shoulder just as the doorbell rang. "Welcome," he greeted, opening the door to Heidi and Alora.

"Thank you for inviting us," Heidi returned, stepping into the house. Alora followed her, making her move straight for Toby.

Toby cringed inside; however, remembering his mission of finding out what kind of trouble his new neighbour might be in, Toby suffered through the child-mauling. *Of course, the kid probably thinks she's giving me love. Little does she know I'm not a typical cat, and, just for your info, kid, most cats prefer to be coddled on their time, not human time!*

Tessa appeared in the doorway. "Shall I take the chicken out of the oven, Jack?" she asked. Then, noticing Heidi and Alora, "You must be Jack's new neighbours … welcome," Tessa said, coming forward with an extended hand. She threw Jack a look.

Jack grinned sheepishly. "Right … let me get you all introduced here—Heidi and Alora, my new neighbours … Tessa, my friend."

Tessa raised her eyebrows. *Friend … oh, Jack … I thought we were past the friend's title!* Smiling, Tessa gripped Heidi's hand in welcome. Turning to Jack, "I think everything else is ready. Just need to carve the chicken."

Jack took his cue and disappeared into the kitchen to tend to the chicken. Toby, having had enough of the kid for now, followed.

Ten minutes later, Jack called the ladies into the kitchen. "Supper's served."

Once everyone's plates were filled, and the humans were about to start eating, Toby went and sat by his dish and meowed, reminding Jack that he'd forgotten something. Tessa laughed as Jack got up and made his way to the cupboard where he kept the cat food.

With supper finished, everyone but Jack retired to the living room. "I'll stay and clean up while you ladies get to know each other," Jack offered.

Toby would much rather have stayed in the kitchen with Jack, but Alora kept calling for him to follow her. *Okay … okay … what I don't do for the sake of a client … I think the kid and her mother require help … time will tell. If my instincts prove wrong, they'll be seeing the tip of my tail!* Toby jumped up to his usual spot on the back of the couch, and Alora snatched up the place beneath him, kneeling and facing Toby instead of sitting correctly.

Heidi and Tessa sat opposite each other, and for a few moments, the only sound in the room was Toby's purring. Of course, he was just doing that for effect, to appease Alora. Finally, Tessa opened the conversation. As a police profiler, she knew how to question someone to get to the bottom of the issues at hand. Jack had filled Tessa in that his new neighbour could be in trouble.

Tessa cleared her throat and began: "Have you always lived in Brantford?"

A warning bell went off in Heidi's head. She'd have to be careful with how much of her past she revealed. "No," she finally said, offering no more.

"So what brings you to our fair city … a job?"

"Not really … no…" Heidi stumbled over her answer.

"You must have family here, then?"

This woman is too nosey… "No, it's just Alora and me." Realizing that Tessa needed an answer and probably would keep probing until she got one, Heidi elaborated. "I had to move out of my place in Hamilton … owner was selling … I saw this ad for the house here in Brantford. Hamilton was getting too big for me. I thought of bringing Alora and Bear here when I saw the place—a quiet street and a big yard—it looked like a good place for us." Heidi didn't need to tell Tessa that it was Lorenzo who had located the house for her.

"What area did you live in Hamilton? The city is spreading out in so many directions."

"Downtown," Heidi answered quickly, not offering an exact local.

Tessa smiled and decided to change the subject. "Alora must be about five?" she asked, raising her eyebrows.

Heidi nodded.

"Has she started school yet?"

"I homeschool."

"Nice." Tessa could tell Heidi was being evasive, not wanting to give up too much personal information. "A lot of families are going that route now," she added, not wanting Heidi to feel she was judging her homeschooling decision. "What made you decide to homeschool?" Tessa asked nonchalantly.

Heidi scowled, tired of all the personal queries. "You ask a lot of questions."

Tessa smiled. "Just trying to get to know you, Heidi. If you want, ask anything about me that you like."

Toby was closely watching what was transpiring. He could tell Heidi didn't want to talk about herself. *She's definitely hiding something!*

Heidi took Tessa up on her offer, targeting in on exactly who the woman questioning her was. "Okay then, what do you do?"

"I'm a freelance profiler," Tessa smiled. "Semi-retired, actually. The police call on me on a need basis." She paused. "That's how I met Jack. Some mysterious deaths were happening in Brantford, and the police were baffled." Tessa looked over at Toby, who was suffering through a back scratch from Alora. "Well, I guess I should say the police were baffled, but Toby had the whole thing figured out. He just had to figure out a way to tell Jack and the police. Toby is quite the detective, you know."

"Really?" Heidi couldn't help smiling at the thought of a cat being a detective. "So what was going on?" she asked curiously, happy the conversation was steering away from her.

"Well," Tessa started to explain, "A brother and sister moved next door to the house where you're living now, and they were quite disturbed by things that had happened in the past, especially the brother. The young man was poisoning people he thought were insulting him, or simply not being courteous. He would send them an email, telling them to repent the error of their ways, but he wasn't giving them time to do so. He'd slipped over the edge of sanity. As I said, Toby figured everything out, and he saved the last victim by jumping off the roof of the gym down the street and knocking the protein drink out of the victim's hand."

Alora had been listening intently to Tessa, and her first fear was for Toby when Tessa had said that Toby had jumped off the roof of a building. "Was Toby hurt?" she asked.

"Well, yes, he was hurt pretty badly. But, as you can see, he's quite recovered from the ordeal. So much so that a few months later, Toby solved another crime."

"Wow!" Alora's eyes lit up, and she reached up and gave Toby a hug and a kiss. "I knew you were special, Toby!"

You bet I'm special, little lady … you have no idea just how special I am. You can let go of me now, though. Toby wiggled out of Alora's grasp, and having had enough of child-mauling, jumped down from the couch and made a beeline to the kitchen to check on what Jack was doing.

Alora was about to race after Toby, but Heidi gave her a look. "Leave the kitty, sweetheart," she said in a firm tone. Alora pouted and slumped back on the couch. Then, turning back to Tessa, Heidi asked another question. "Where are the brother and sister now?"

"The brother is in prison, and the sister moved away a short time ago so she could be closer to her brother." Tessa didn't feel it was necessary to tell Heidi about the state of affairs Emma had gotten herself into, and then out of, thanks to Jack, who hired a good lawyer for her. There had always been something about what had gone down that kept niggling at Tessa, telling her that the police officer had it right. Emma was guilty of something, but that something wasn't proven beyond a reasonable doubt.

Heidi shivered. She hadn't thought about who might have lived in the house previous to her. Why should she? *I wonder what the sister did … obviously something Tessa doesn't want to discuss … this profiler woman thinks she knows me and can fool me as well … not on her life. She has no idea what I've been through.* Heidi's discomfort level was rising, and she decided it was time to take her leave.

She hated to eat and run, especially since her actual host was just joining the group in the living room. She stood and looked at her watch. “I hate to leave so soon, Jack, but I must get Alora to bed,” she gave out her excuse.

“I don’t want to go home,” Alora complained.

“It’s time, sweetheart,” Heidi’s tone suggested she wouldn’t tolerate further delay. Heidi reached over to Alora and took her daughter by the hand and made her way to the front door.

Jack followed her and opened the door for his guests. “I apologize for my delay in the kitchen. I hope you enjoyed the meal tonight and will maybe come back on the weekend for lunch—so you won’t have to leave so soon, and we’ll be able to get to know each other better.”

Heidi didn’t want to seem ungrateful; Jack looked like a nice man. But Tessa, well, she was just too nosey for Heidi’s liking. She had no desire to return for a meal at Jack’s house if Tessa was going to be present to drill her with more questions about her life. So, she smiled sweetly at Jack and said, “I’ll take a rain-check on this weekend; I promised Alora we’d do something special.”

Alora opened her mouth to protest, but Heidi squeezed her daughter’s hand, shutting off any comments that might refute what she’d just told Jack. Toby, who had just joined the people, noticed everything and was not impressed. *I wonder if Heidi is in trouble, if she doesn’t deserve whatever is coming to her.*

15

Cain was beginning to have doubts about Pete's loyalty, despite having been recommended by Lorenzo, whom he considered one of the most loyal employees he'd ever hired. Cain ran a hand through his hair, then leaned on the sink and stared out the window toward the back building. Pete was leaning against the side of the structure, a cell phone glued to his ear. Cain wished he could read lips.

Pete finished his conversation, shoved the cell phone into his pant pocket, and took off toward his car. Cain noticed how frustrated Pete seemed to be. Cain pulled out his cell phone and made a call.

"Mitch, here," the voice on the other end of the line answered the ring.

"Are you busy right now?" Cain knew he didn't have to identify himself to Mitch.

"A little. Collecting a debt for you, boss. I'm on my way out to your place. Thought you might like to make the final decision about what to do with someone who tries to double-cross you."

Cain laughed—not a pleasant sound, though. "Okay, then. As soon as you get here, lock the guy up in the cottage behind the building, then come and see me."

"You got it, boss." Mitch shut off the Bluetooth, turned, and glanced at Cameron, who was lying on the backseat of the vehicle. "Boss wants to see you, Cam."

Cameron's eyes were wild with fear. All of his well-laid plans were going up in smoke, as he assumed he would be soon as he handed over the money. The one salvation he felt was that Mitch, even though he'd terrified his family, had not harmed them. His son, Devlin, had peed his pants on the way to the park, but Mitch had been true to his word and let the kid go—with a warning to go straight home to his mommy and not speak to anyone along the way, or Daddy would come to harm. Cameron couldn't say a word in return. His mouth was taped shut.

Mitch turned onto the long, treed laneway to Cain's property, and drove around to the back of the big building behind the house, where there was a thick grove of trees. Mitch put the car in park, got out and pulled Cameron out of the back seat, slinging him easily over his shoulder, like a sack of potatoes. He pushed his way through the trees to the small wood cabin. Kicking open the door, Mitch deposited Cameron on a cot situated in the far corner. He left without a word and drove up to the house.

Cain was waiting for him in the kitchen, a glass of Scotch in his hand. Mitch heard the ice cubes clinking as Cain swirled the liquid gold. "What's up, boss?"

"What do you think of Pete?" Cain drove straight to the point.

"Never really thought about him at all," Mitch replied, puzzled with Cain's question.

"Something about him doesn't sit right with me," Cain continued thoughtfully. "I want you to look into his past..."

"I thought your good friend, Lorenzo, recommended Pete to take his place?" Mitch interrupted.

"Indeed, he did." Cain gulped his drink and set the glass on the table. "You know, I've been doing a lot of thinking about things. Lorenzo didn't look pleased when he walked in on me that day, teaching my wife a lesson. It wasn't much longer after that when Lorenzo came to me and said he needed to retire; he'd been thinking about it for a long time. Told me he was getting old. I said I was sorry to see him go and asked if he could recommend someone to take his place. He said he'd think about it, and it wasn't until a few days later that he introduced me to Pete.

"I trusted Lorenzo … many times, even with my life. But, you know, this Pete, he comes here and takes over Jennifer's walks, and then, poof! She's gone." Cain turned and stared out the window. "I want you to follow him whenever you can, as well. He received a phone call and then took off from here a while ago, like a maniac. I don't like it."

"What do you want me to do if I find the guy doing something untoward?" Mitch asked.

"Don't do anything. Just come and tell me. I'll decide then what to do."

"Okay. Now, what do you want me to do with the guy in the cabin?"

"Has he indicated how he's going to get the money?"

"Nope."

"Let him stew for a bit."

Mitch went to the cupboard and retrieved a glass and poured himself some water. "I think Cameron knows as soon as he tells us how to get the money, or he just gets it for us, he's a goner. So I don't think he cares."

"He'll care if he knows that not telling us will cause damage to his family." Cain hesitated, then, making his decision, "I'll deal with the man in the cabin. You get on checking out Pete for me." Another hesitation. "By the way, you saw Jennifer?"

"I did."

"Did she see you?"

"No. She was busy in her backyard with the kid. Had the dog with her, and looks like she has herself a cat, too. You want me to do something about her, too?"

Cain shook his head. "No. There's plenty of time to deal with Jennifer. I don't want her spooked." Cain picked up his glass and went to the freezer and added more ice to it before pouring another shot of Scotch. It was Mitch's cue to leave.

Cameron was praying for a deliverer when he heard the crunch of footsteps approaching his prison. He had an inkling, though, that whoever it was, wasn't a friend. The door creaked open. Cameron didn't want to look; he squeezed his eyes tight. A harsh laugh penetrated the silence and the sound of a chair scraping across the floor.

"Closing your eyes is not going to save you," the voice said. "Open up and face your music."

Cameron slowly opened his eyes and stared into the eyes of the devil. Cain's eyes were bloodshot—from booze and lack of sleep. His hair was dishevelled. His beard showed at least three day's growth.

Cain reached over and ripped the tape from Cameron's mouth. "There now," his voice grated, "isn't that better. You can get your words out easier," Cain mocked.

Cameron licked his lips nervously. *This guy must be the boss. Shit! No way out of this mess I created.*

"Mitch tells me you have a nice family," Cain began, a hint of a future threat in his words. The intimidation followed quickly. "I'd hate to see anything happen to them. How about you, Cameron? Do you love your family enough to give up what isn't yours? What never was yours? To keep them safe?" Cain chuckled and leaned forward in the chair. "Tell me what you did with the money you owe me, Cameron."

Cameron remained silent.

"Do you know what happened to Sam—the man you directly owed the money to?"

Cameron shook his head.

"I'd call him and let you talk to him, but something tells me—a little bird—Sam wouldn't be able to answer the phone. Get my drift?"

Cameron's eyes widened in fear. Sweat broke out across his brow. He swallowed hard, knowing that no matter what he did, he was doomed. The least he would be able to do was save his family. Cameron dug deep for the courage to speak: "I'll tell you how to get the money on one condition ... you have to promise you won't harm my family. They had nothing to do with what I did."

Cain laughed. "Do you actually think you're in a position to negotiate with me?"

"I know I'm doomed," Cameron stated. "I just want my family to be safe."

"Here's what we're going to do," Cain stated. "I'm going to take the restraint off your ankles, and we're going walk to my office. I assume we have to use a computer to access the money?"

Cameron nodded affirmation, the only thing he was capable of doing at the moment.

Cain took a knife out from an ankle holster and cut the tape from around Cameron's ankles, then helped his prisoner to his feet and shoved him toward the door. It took a few moments for Cameron to get his balance; his feet were tingling from lack of circulation.

When they reached the front of the large office building, Cain took out his key ring and opened the door.

He shoved Cameron inside. "This way," Cain pointed to a room on the far side of the building.

Cameron looked around and couldn't believe his eyes. There was floor to ceiling racks in the place, filled with boxes. Knowing what little he knew, Cameron assumed most of the cartons had illegal street drugs in them. *This guy must be worth a fortune ... and he wants the few grand I owe him! Life means nothing to a guy like this. Nothing! Oh, God, I can't believe I got myself into such a mess! No way out for me.* Cameron stopped at the office door and waited for Cain to open it. Once inside, Cain directed Cameron to the computer desk. The computers were already running.

"So, Cameron. Let's do this."

"My family will be safe?" Cameron dared to ask.

"We'll talk once my money is in my account—not yours."

Cameron realized he had no choice. If he didn't give up the money, he and his family were done for. If he gave it up, there was a slim chance they would live. For the next ten minutes, Cameron ran Cain through the process of connecting with his island account, and when he completed the transaction, Cain leaned back in the chair and grinned.

"Now, that wasn't so bad, was it?"

Cameron was so nervous about what was going to happen next that he couldn't say a word.

Cain stood and shoved Cameron toward the door. "Let's take a walk, Cameron. I'm sure you need to stretch your legs a bit more. I want to show you something."

Probably the tip of his knife against my throat, or maybe the place where he buries the bodies of people who cross him. Oh, God! I feel like puking. Cameron stumbled out the door.

Cain laughed. "Don't be nervous, Cameron. I haven't decided what I'm going to do with you yet." Cain led the way through the aisles of boxes, explaining to Cameron what was in each row. After half an hour of listening to the tedious rendition of the entire operation, Cain stopped at the outside door. "You're awfully quiet, Cameron. What do you think of all this?" Without allowing Cameron to answer, Cain continued. "Something like this isn't built overnight. It also isn't built by allowing guys like you to take advantage of the operation. Wouldn't you agree?"

Cameron nodded, still unable to speak.

Cain opened the door and motioned for Cameron to go first. It was already dark out, and it couldn't have been a blacker night. Not a star visible in the sky. The moon was hiding behind thick rain clouds. Cameron waited for the blow to hit, and was surprised when it didn't. Cain pushed him in the direction of the cabin where Mitch had first taken him.

Maybe this guy isn't going to kill me. Then again, maybe Mitch is waiting in the cabin, and he's going to do the deed. I doubt it that this man—the boss—would dirty his hands; he has men like Mitch to do that for him! No salvation for me … should I keep begging for my family?—, I have to. Cameron reached into his gut and, once again, asked for the safety of his family. "I gave you the money, mister, and I can't tell you how sorry I am that I tried to double-cross you. I understand how this works, but before you do me, I just want my last thoughts to be that I saved my family from premature death."

Cain studied the man in front of him, thinking he could use him. After all, the guy loved his family and would do anything to protect them, and Cain was down a contact, Mitch having disposed of Sam. However, Cain wanted to think it over before making his final decision. He'd let

Cameron stew over what was going to happen to him until tomorrow. Cain opened the cabin door and shoved Cameron through the opening.

16

Heidi tucked Alora into bed and then went downstairs to the living room. She flicked on the television, and Bear came and laid down at her feet. The dog looked up at her with dog-eyes.

"You saw the car, too, didn't you, Bear?"

Bear wagged his tail affirmatively.

"I'm going to have to contact Lorenzo and tell him I think we've been compromised. I hate to do this to Alora again, and so soon. She seems happier here than anywhere we've been. Maybe, I should talk to our neighbour and Tessa; after all, they are law enforcement. Maybe, it's time to stop running and let the authorities know what I know. We need to take Cain down before he ruins too many more lives." Heidi closed her eyes and thought back to her last couple of months at the country property...

> Lorenzo had finally told Heidi his plans. He was going to give his notice soon, and there would be someone new taking over his position. "I've handpicked this guy to recommend to Cain. His name's Pete, and we go back a long way."
>
> "What if Cain won't hire him?" Heidi asked. "He's suspicious about everything nowadays."
>
> "Well, I look at it this way ... Cain trusts me with you, and I've never given him any reason not to trust me."

“Isn’t he going to wonder all of a sudden why you are quitting?”

Lorenzo had run his hand across his beard. “See this, Jennifer? … I mean, Heidi. That’s what I’m going to call you from now on—your new name. This beard is full of gray hair. I’m getting on in years, and I’ve put away enough of a nest egg to live quite comfortably until I die. Cain will understand. He once told me he was going to retire before fifty. He’ll understand me wanting to do so at sixty-five.”

Heidi still wasn’t sure that would be the case, but she nodded and said, “I hope so … for both our sakes.” She paused. “So, what’s the plan?”

“I’ve filled Pete in on what is going on here. He was surprised I was even working for such a man that would beat a woman and threaten a little child with the same. I told Pete that Cain hadn’t always been like that. You know, something changed in him when he started raking in the money…”

“You stayed working for Cain, though, even when you knew what he was selling,” Heidi pointed out. “That part of his life hadn’t changed. How could you even begin working for him if you knew he was selling drugs?”

“Truthfully … Cain didn’t always sell drugs; when we met, he dealt in antiquities and did quite well with them. That’s when I started working for him. However, he met up with a guy by the name of Rubio Cantinelli, and it was not too long after that Cain began to change. Rubio was in antiquities, as well. Only, I guess, he was also importing drugs inside the treasures.”

"What happened to Rubio? Or is he still around ...a partner, perhaps?"

Lorenzo looked away for a moment, cleared his throat, and, "He just disappeared ... about two years after he and Cain went into business together." Lorenzo called over to Alora to be careful and not to pull on Bear's tail. Then, "Let's get back to the issue at hand, Heidi. As I said, I have filled Pete in on everything. All the details for your escape and concealment afterward have been worked out, and Pete will execute my plan right down to the minutest detail.

"Nothing's going to happen until about a month after I leave, you're going to have to be patient. Do you understand? I cannot emphasize enough the importance of you playing this out as though nothing is changed. Cain is perceptive. He'll pick up on anything out of the ordinary." Lorenzo appeared nervous about what he'd put into action.

"I can't thank you enough, Lorenzo. I won't let you down. If you say this Pete can be trusted, I believe you." Heidi paused before asking the question that was on her mind. "Is Bear part of this?"

Lorenzo smiled for the first time during their conversation. "Of course. If I didn't include him, once Cain discovered you gone, he'd destroy Bear. In one small way, I think he knows how much the dog means to Alora, and, despite what Cain is, he has a soft spot for his daughter."

"But, quite obviously, not her mother," Heidi said bitterly.

A week later, Lorenzo was gone, and Pete showed up the next day to take her outside.

Heidi opened her eyes to the eleven o'clock newscaster talking about another shooting in Hamilton. She rubbed her eyes, shut the television off, and stood. Bear got up and nudged his mistress with his nose. "Want to stretch your legs for a few minutes, eh?"

Bear raced to the back door. Heidi sat on the back step and watched Bear sprint around the yard. He let out a couple of sharp barks, and Heidi quickly shushed him. After ten minutes, Heidi called Bear over to her. He placed his head on her lap while she stroked his back. "It's not over, you know, my friend. Cain won't let me go; I'm never going to be free of him. Not while he's still so close. Hamilton is still too near to here for comfort. I think I'll talk to Lorenzo tomorrow and see what he suggests."

The only sound, for a few minutes, was that of the night crickets. Finally, Heidi stood: "Come on, boy. Time to call it a night."

17

After breakfast, Heidi sent Alora and Bear into the backyard to play. As she opened the back door for them, Heidi was surprised to see Toby sitting on the stoop. "Well, good morning, Toby. How nice of you to come by. I guess you're here to see Alora?" Heidi smiled, despite the rough night of reminiscing she'd been through.

Well, if you want to think I'm here for the kid, that's okay with me. I'm actually here to see if I can discover what's going on with you, lady … and now that I know the dog and I are most likely on the same team, and that he's not going to take my head off like the other mutt that used to live here would have, I can come and go with more confidence. Toby meowed and rubbed around Alora's legs. She squealed in delight.

"If you guys need anything, just call … bark … meow!" Heidi grinned and went back into the house to make her phone call. She made her way upstairs to her room and dug in the back of her top dresser drawer for the cell phone she used to call Lorenzo. Sitting on the edge of her bed, Heidi dialled the number.

After six rings, a female voice answered. "Hello."

Heidi was startled. In the three years since she'd left Cain, no one but Lorenzo had ever answered his phone. "Who are you?" Heidi asked cautiously.

A long pause on the other end gave Heidi room for even more concern. Her hand started to shake, and Heidi felt as though she were going to throw up. Something was wrong. Just as Heidi was about to hang up, "I am Officer Lawrence of the Brantford police … now, I ask again, who are you? Why are you calling this number? Do you know Lorenzo?"

The shock of the question made Heidi drop the phone. It crashed on the floor, and the screen broke into pieces. Heidi fell to her knees and burst into tears. *What the hell am I going to do now?*

Pete tore out of the laneway to Cain's property after his phone call with Lorenzo. Pete and Lorenzo had been friends for years, and Pete could tell by Lorenzo's tone that there was something terribly wrong.

Lorenzo had taken up residence in Brantford in a small upper apartment in an old house on Dufferin Avenue. He wanted to be close to Heidi, but keep his locale secret from her. Pete took the back way—Hwy 52—into Brantford, going through the downtown to Brant Avenue. He admired the high school, B.C.I., as he passed it, then turned left onto Richmond Street, and then right onto Dufferin. Halfway down the street, Pete saw the police cars, lights flashing, blocking the road. Two of the cruisers were sitting in the driveway of a two-story house; two others were parked across the street, blocking it. A siren permeated the air as it raced toward the scene, pulling up in front of the house.

Pete pulled over to the side and parked, keeping his car idling. He watched the paramedics get out of the ambulance and head around to the back entrance of the house. Lorenzo had told Pete that the access to his apartment was behind the house. Pete glanced at the number of the house he was parked beside, and his heart skipped more than a couple of beats!

"This has to be Lorenzo's place," Pete muttered. He continued watching until he saw the paramedics exiting the house, followed by three police officers. The body on the gurney was in a body-bag. "Damn!" Pete hit the steering wheel. "The bugger's gone and got himself killed … or, maybe he's had a heart attack. I've told him to watch what he ate, but he wouldn't listen to me … however, if it was just a heart attack, why would so many police be here?"

Pete noticed a couple of neighbours standing close to Lorenzo's place. He decided to take a walk and see if he could get any valuable information from them. He shut the engine off, got out of his car, and sauntered down the sidewalk toward the women.

"Hello, ladies," Pete greeted them with a charming smile.

The elder of the two turned and scowled at the interruption. The younger smiled at him and said hello back.

Pete zeroed in on her for the information he was seeking. "What happened here?" he inquired.

"Murder, I believe," the young woman replied. "I was out in my garage … I live next door … when I heard two loud bangs. I rushed outside just in time to see a car race off…"

"What kind of car?" Pete interrupted.

"I'm not up much on car types … it was dark, black, I think, and big. Fancy." She paused and gave Pete another smile. "I called the police and told them I thought they needed to get here A.S.A.P. I said I thought someone could be in trouble … maybe even shot."

"I see whoever they brought out must have lived upstairs," Pete pointed out. "Did you know who lived there?"

The older woman spoke up this time. "Not well. An older man. Hasn't lived there that long. Kept to himself pretty much, but he helped me the other day when I couldn't get my car started."

Pete stared at the back of the ambulance; the paramedics were loading the body. *It certainly has to be Lorenzo. Damn, what do I do now? I'll have to wait until later to try and get into his apartment to see if Lorenzo left me any clue as to what he wanted.*

"I've never seen you around here," the older woman said, bringing Pete out of his thoughts. "Are you visiting someone on this street?" she added.

Pete wasn't about to say why he was there and that he probably knew the victim. "Just taking this street to miss all the heavy Brant Avenue traffic," he replied. "I love looking at old homes too, and the different architecture used throughout the years."

"Oh, yes, they are beautiful, aren't they? It's what attracted my husband and me to the area. Unfortunately, he didn't get to enjoy our place for long; he passed away from cancer a year after we moved here," the younger woman batted her eyes at Pete.

Pete smiled sympathetically. "I'm sorry for your loss, ma'am." *Looks like you're on the hunt for a replacement, but it won't be me, lady!* Pete noticed a female officer heading towards him and the ladies. He had no intention of being questioned by the police. "Well, ladies, I guess I'll be on my way; I'll just have to turn around and make my way back to Brant Ave. Been nice chatting with you."

"Likewise," the younger woman articulated. "By the way, we didn't get your name," she called out to his back.

Pete pretended he didn't hear her. He quickened his pace, got in his car, did a three-point turn, and drove away from the scene.

"Who was the gentleman that was just here?" the female police officer questioned, approaching the two women.

"No idea," the older woman replied. "We didn't get his name."

"Said he was just trying to avoid the Brant Ave traffic by taking the scenic route," the younger female added.

"So, what you're saying is that he doesn't live on this street?" the officer asked.

"No," the younger woman answered.

"Which one of you called the police?" the policewoman asked, remembering why she'd approached the neighbourhood watch.

The older woman had enough of all the excitement. "Wasn't me," she informed. "I need to get home; my dog will be anxious to get out for a walk."

The officer let her go and turned to the younger woman. "I need to get your statement."

"No problem. My house is next door to the victim's if you'd like to take it there."

"Sure, let's do that."

18

Cameron was beginning to drift off to sleep when he heard footsteps approaching—more than one set. *I'm done ... sorry God ... maybe I can get some forgiveness if you're in a generous mood, but, if not, please protect my family. My wife ... she attends mass every week, and my kids are innocents—too young to pay for their father's mistakes.*

The door swung open, and two men stepped inside—Mitch and Cain. Mitch walked over to Cameron and roughly got him to his feet, shoved him across the room and pushed him into a chair at a table situated in the middle of the room. Cain positioned himself at the other end of the table. Mitch stood behind Cameron, his hands folded behind his back.

He's going to take me from behind, I bet. Cameron's hands began to shake. *Make it quick, please.*

Cain opened the conversation. "I've given your situation much thought, Cameron, and I want you to know that I'm not in the business of snuffing out people. So, I am going to make you a proposal." Cain paused for effect. "Sam isn't going to be available to look after my business in Brantford, so I need a man I can trust to take over. You could be the person I'm looking for."

Another pause. Cain leaned forward, his elbows on the table, his hands laced palm to palm. "Are you my man?" Cain asked. "Oh, excuse me..." Cain motioned to Mitch, "Take that tape off our guest's mouth."

Cameron screamed in pain as the tape ripped away. He would have rubbed his hand across his lips, but his wrists were still behind his back.

"Now that you can answer me," Cain resumed, "Are you going to be my man?"

Cameron still couldn't speak; his nerves were raw. He nodded instead.

"Speak up!" Cain ordered.

Finally, "Yes … anything you want. I'll do anything."

"Okay, then. Here it is. You will do whatever I ask, and your family will remain safe. However, you will have no contact with any member of your family until I say you're clear to do so. And, to ensure your wife doesn't decide to do something stupid, she and your children will be removed to a housing of my choice and will be under 24-hour watch."

"What about my kid's schooling?" Cameron dared to ask.

"I'll provide them a tutor," came Cain's well-thought-out answer.

"Where will I live?"

"Here."

"What about my house. It isn't good to leave a place empty—vandalism, you know." Cameron was trying to cover all his bases.

"Already sold." Cain leaned back and grinned. "So, what do you say? Are you in?"

Cameron stared at the table. *Do I have a choice? At the least, I need to keep my family safe.* "Yeah … I'm in."

Cain nodded to Mitch. "Remove the man's restraints. Take him up to the house and clean him up, then feed him. Once done, bring him back to my office and I'll give him his first assignment."

"Will do, boss," Mitch said as he cut the tape from Cameroon's wrists and ankles.

Two hours later, Cameron was clean and fed, sitting across from Cain, waiting to hear his fate. *Better than being dead … I think.*

19

Heidi paced in her kitchen, trying to decide the best way to approach Jack and ask for his help. The radio was playing in the background. Suddenly, her ear tuned in on what the newscaster was saying…

There was a shooting this morning at an apartment on Dufferin Avenue, here in Brantford. The victim expired at the crime scene. The police are withholding his identity until a next of kin can be notified. So far, the police have no suspect or motive.

Heidi stopped and choked back a sob. "It has to be Lorenzo. Now, what do I do? You only told me what I needed to do or where I needed to go at the last minute, Lorenzo. Have you filled Pete in on all the details—or is he dead too? Or, is he the one who killed you—turned on you, deciding Cain had more to offer?"

Bear was barking up a storm in the backyard. "I'm going to have to do something about your noise, dog!" Heidi grumbled as she made her way out to the yard. She was about to yell at Bear to stop when she noticed his reason for causing a ruckus. Heidi caught the tail-end of a black limo as it was picking up speed after slowing down in front of her house. Bear was at the fence, barking, and strangely, Toby was right beside him, staring in the direction the car had gone, the hair on his back standing straight up, his tail fluffed and switching angrily. Alora was kneeling between the two animals, a hand on each of their backs.

Bear turned when he heard Heidi approaching. “Looks as though trouble is catching up with us, boy,” Heidi said, stopping by the trio. “Let’s go inside.” Heidi directed the trio toward the house. “You’re welcome, too, Toby,” she added when she noticed the cat hesitating.

Toby’d had enough of playing with Alora; however, there were still some issues he felt he needed to investigate. *Well, I guess it won’t hurt for a bit … might find something valuable. Maybe I can snoop around the house––as long as the mutt doesn’t interfere.* Toby followed the crew inside.

Heidi was preparing a snack for Alora; Bear was lapping up some water from his dish. Toby sat in the middle of the room, searching for a clue as to what was going on.

The chime of a cell phone broke into the calm. Heidi wiped her hands on a towel and walked to the living room. Toby followed discretely and settled behind a chair where he was out of sight, but could still hear Heidi’s conversation—at least her half.

“Hello.”

“Heidi?”

“Yes … who … oh, is this Pete?”

“Yeah. I’m afraid I have some bad news.”

“So, it’s true then. I heard something on the radio.”

“I’m pretty sure. I was on my way to see Lorenzo, but the police were all over the place. I never saw the body the paramedics brought out.”

“What do I do now?” Heidi decided to tell Pete about the limo that had driven by her house more than once. “I think Cain knows where I am; a black limo drove by yesterday and again today.”

“Crap!” Pete hesitated. “I’m going to try and get into the apartment and see if Lorenzo left me any clues,” Pete added.

"Be careful," Heidi warned. "Are you going back out to Cain's?"

"I don't think so. If Cain got to Lorenzo, he probably knows about me. I'll go somewhere I can hide out until I figure out a plan."

"Pete…"

"Yeah?"

"Thank you."

"No problem. I'll stay in touch. If you don't hear from me by tomorrow night, get out of the house." The line went dead.

Heidi was pale and shaking uncontrollably as she laid her cell phone on the coffee table. She sat down on the couch and put her head in her hands. Toby noticed Heidi's shoulders shaking and heard choking sobs coming from her direction. Toby had learned a couple things: Pete seemed to be a friend … Cain, not so much … Heidi was aware someone was watching her place. *But how do I tell Jack this? I am cursed sometimes, being a speechless animal. Only so many things I can communicate with humans!*

Heidi finally collected herself, wiped away her tears, and returned to the kitchen. Toby decided it was time to leave, so he went to the back door and meowed to be let out. *When I get home, I'm going to set up a vigil and watch for that black car. Even Bear doesn't like it.*

After Toby left, Heidi set Alora up in the living room with one of her favourite television programs, "Peppa Pig" before heading upstairs to her room. Going into her closet, Heidi pulled out a box and set it on her bed. The contents of the box contained damning evidence against Cain.

Heidi pulled out a large envelope and dumped its contents on the quilt. She picked up the pictures one by one, sorting them into piles. Lorenzo had snuck her a camera before he'd left. Heidi sifted through the ones that were already on the memory card, ones Lorenzo must have taken showing the operation inside the vast warehouse. There were a lot more men who were going to go down once she went to the police with the pictures; however, Heidi had to be sure everything was in line before she did that. She was willing to take a chance and tell Jack some things, but she was going to hold some things back. Heidi decided she wouldn't show Jack any of this evidence for now.

Had Toby stuck around, he would have witnessed this scene and had a better chance of getting Jack to discover who was after their new neighbour.

20

Lorenzo drove slowly down the rutted lane to the location he'd secured as a safe-house. He'd been around people like Cain long enough to know that no one place was safe. Once inside the cabin, Lorenzo checked the wood stove for wood. It was full. He took a few pieces of newspaper from a pile, scrunched them up, and shoved them under some of the wood chunks, then lit them with a match. Soon there was a crackling fire going, and Lorenzo shut the wood stove's door. Next, he checked the oil lamp and a stash of candles he'd hoarded last time he'd checked on the place.

The cabin was void of any modern conveniences, so the woodstove served for both heat and cooking. Lorenzo was starving. He dug into a big box in the corner and pulled out a can of beef stew. After he finished his meal, Lorenzo stepped outside and lit a cigarette. As he puffed away, he thought back to the past few tumultuous hours he'd endured...

> Lorenzo's phone call to Pete had been to say they needed to meet, and the sooner, the better. Lorenzo held back from Pete what he felt was going on. For a week, Lorenzo suspected someone was following him. Pete had said he would leave immediately.
>
> Twenty minutes after calling Pete, Lorenzo noticed a black car park across the street. A man

dressed all in black got out and walked toward Lorenzo's house. "Damn!" Lorenzo grabbed his getaway bag and set it by the door, ready for a quick departure if the need arose. He walked quickly to his desk and took his gun out of the hidden compartment in the bottom drawer and secured the silencer on the barrel. Then he waited in his bedroom, watching through a two-way mirror he'd had installed.

A few minutes later, Lorenzo heard the lock jiggle, and the door squeaked open. Despite the intruder trying to be quiet, Lorenzo detected footsteps. As the man moved around the apartment, his gun drawn, Lorenzo knew what he was going to have to do, and he'd hoped he could accomplish the deed before the guy fired off his gun. Unfortunately, that isn't the way it played out.

The two-way mirror only covered a small area of the apartment, and without warning, the intruder kicked in the bedroom door and fired two shots at the bed. Lorenzo had fixed the bedding so that it would appear he was taking a nap. Lorenzo fired once, catching the man off-guard. As the trespasser turned and faced Lorenzo, his eyes wide with shock, his mouth open in disbelief, Lorenzo fired another shot, and the assailant crumpled to the ground. Quickly, Lorenzo picked the man up and plunked him on the bed. He dug around in the man's pocket, found the car keys, then left, grabbing his bag on the way out the door.

Lorenzo moved fast for a man of his stature and was soon taking off down the street, hoping no one had seen him leave the house. When he felt he was far enough away, Lorenzo pulled over and parked the car on the side of the road. He reached over to the glove compartment and dug around inside.

"Bingo!" Lorenzo pulled out a plastic cardholder and flipped it open. "Tomas Abila." A business card fell out of the holder—C Enterprises. "Cain. I should have known he'd figure things out sooner or later. Well, he's underestimated me. Soon as I get out to the cabin, I'll contact Pete and make sure he doesn't go back to Cain's place, and that he warns Heidi. I don't want anyone other than Pete knowing I am still alive."

Lorenzo took out a unique tool that could detect "bugs" and walked all around the car. Under the back bumper, he found a transmitter. Lorenzo snapped it off and ground it onto the sidewalk with his heel. He got back into the car and pulled out into the traffic and took off out of the city.

Stamping his cigarette out, Lorenzo returned to the cabin. He dug around in his bag and pulled out a cell phone, one of the many burners he had on hand. After dialling Pete's number, Lorenzo took a seat on the love seat and stretched out his legs. It had been a long day and he was exhausted. Pete answered after the sixth ring.

"Hello."

"Pete … Lorenzo, here."

"Lorenzo! My God, man … I thought you were dead! I watched as the paramedics brought you out of the house in a body bag."

"Wasn't me."

"Who, then?"

"The guy Cain sent to kill me. He must have finally figured out that I helped his wife escape, and if he knows that, he will probably figure out quite quickly that you were my inside man." Lorenzo took a moment before asking his question. "Have you talked to Heidi?"

"Yes. I told her I thought you were dead."

"Keep it that way for now. The fewer people who know I'm alive, the better. If Cain knows where his wife is now, goodness knows what he'll do. He might even go after Alora and take her from Heidi."

"That would be my guess," Pete affirmed Lorenzo's suspicion. "A couple weeks ago, I walked into his office and he was staring at a picture of Alora, taken not long before she and her mom fled. If I were a betting man, I'd say there were tears in his eyes. He must have a heart for something, and it appears that something just might be his daughter."

"Cain has no love for anything but money," Lorenzo stated. "His daughter, in reality, is nothing more than a possession to be used to manipulate Heidi."

"There's something you need to know, Lorenzo," Pete said, his tone becoming serious. "Heidi feels someone's watching her. Cain obviously discovered where she is. He's got people everywhere; told her to be careful, and if she doesn't hear from me by tomorrow night, she's to get out of there. I hope that isn't even too late."

"Yeah." A lengthy pause, then, "Where are you staying?"

"I'm safe, buddy. Don't worry about me. And to set your mind at ease, I'll keep an eye on Heidi and wait for you to tell me what your plans are for her and the kid."

"Okay. Good. I'll call you tomorrow. But first thing in the morning, I want you to pick up a couple more burner phones, and I'll get the numbers from you when you call."

"Got it."

"Take care."

"You too, bud."

Lorenzo decided the best thing he could do now was to get a good sleep. When he woke, he'd be refreshed and able to figure out what to do. "Maybe it's time we take you down, Cain … then Heidi—Jennifer—and Alora wouldn't have to keep running and looking over their shoulders. That's no life for them. And I could get the hell out of here––Pete and I—to that island paradise where I have my money stashed."

Pete stretched out on the king-size bed in the hotel room he'd rented. He picked up the hotel phone, dialled down to room service, and ordered something to eat. Half an hour later, Pete was digging into a steak dinner. A good meal and then a good night's sleep was what he needed now. Tomorrow was another day.

21

Heidi put the items back in the box and returned it to her closet. She heaved a sigh of relief that she'd made her decision to go after Cain. She was tired of running. A good man had lost his life today, all because he was trying to protect her.

"I am better than this. I was a strong woman once. Before Cain. I need to take charge before someone else dies because of me." Heidi left her room and went downstairs and called Jack.

Jack answered on the fourth ring. He sounded sleepy. "Hello."

"Jack, this is Heidi. You said you are a retired policeman, right?"

"Yes."

"I need to talk to you about something exceedingly important. Are you able to come over to my place?"

"When?"

"Now, if possible."

"Okay, give me five minutes."

"I'll meet you in the backyard. I don't want Alora to hear anything of what I'm going to say."

Ten minutes later, Jack entered Heidi's yard. She was sitting on the back step and stood as Jack approached. Heidi extended her hand, taking Jack's in hers. "Thank you, Jack."

"No problem. I had a sense you might have a problem. I'll let you take the lead." Jack motioned back to the step. "Shall we sit?"

Heidi nodded. She heaved a sizeable sigh and began. "My real name is Jennifer, and I am hiding from an evil man. A man who, at one time, swept me off my feet and married me, who I thought was my white knight. However, he turned out to be blacker than anyone I've ever known. He asked me to quit my job, saying we didn't need the money. I held out for a bit, but then he bought this acreage in the country, and we moved there. He pressured me again to quit my job, saying he feared for me with the driving back and forth to the city, especially in the winter. Finally, I conceded.

"However, it didn't end there. My husband began cutting me off from my friends. Then, I discovered I was pregnant, and I couldn't have been happier. I thought my husband would change, but he got worse. He was away more than ever before. Told me he was in sales, but never actually said what he was selling. There was a considerable-sized building behind the house and a lot of cars, big limos, came and went all the time. After Alora was born, I dared to speak back to my husband one day: that was the first time he hit me. Without warning, he locked me in the house, and I was only able to go out for fresh air under guard.

"He had bought Bear for me before all this happened, but when he locked me in the house, he took Bear and kept him out in the building behind our house—the building where he conducted his business. The man who came every day to take me for walks, let Bear out to be with us. I could tell this man had a conscience, but he was an employee and was doing his job. One day, my husband was going to strike Alora, and I stepped between him and my child. I received the beating of my life. I thought I was going to die as I lay on the floor, taking each blow and praying it would be the last. However, the man who walked me happened to come in during this episode, and my husband stopped. You see, up to this point, no one had witnessed firsthand what he was doing to me behind closed doors.

"There was some sort of meeting going on, and my husband's guests had arrived—the reason why my walker had come to get him—so the two men left. However, my walker turned and looked at me, and I could see sympathy in his eyes. I started to formulate an idea in my head, something I would need help with. I rationalized if my walker had any sympathy for me, and for my child, he just might help us to escape the hell we were in." Heidi paused. Reliving all that had happened to her and sharing it with someone who was still primarily a stranger was difficult.

Jack noticed Heidi didn't give away any names in her rendition of what had taken place in her life. "Are you afraid to tell me the names of your husband and anyone connected with him and his business?" Jack asked with an air of concern in his voice.

Heidi looked away, not sure how to answer. "Maybe I've made a mistake telling you all this. Maybe you don't want to get involved with someone like me. You probably don't need this kind of trouble in your life…" Heidi made a move to get up.

Jack reached out a hand and laid it on Heidi's knee. "Stop right there, Heidi. I've worked in law enforcement all my life, and when I retired from the force, whenever the police needed extra help, they called me in." Jack pointed to Toby, who had quietly entered the yard and was sitting on the grass, taking in all that Heidi was saying. "We have solved more than one crime for the police, especially Toby.

He has a nose for these things, strange as that might seem, him being a cat and all. In truth, Toby has sensed something going on with you. Besides the two of us, there is my friend, Tessa. We met when we were working on the Camden Gale case; she's one of the best profilers around."

"Thus, all the questions last night?" Heidi asked knowingly. She'd suspected something when Tessa kept pushing into her past.

Jack chuckled softly. "She can't help it. I told Tessa you might be in some kind of trouble. Toby isn't the only one who can sniff out a damsel in distress. So, I asked Tessa to see if she could get through to you. The reason I stayed and cleaned the kitchen after supper."

"I thought something was up. Reason I left so early," Heidi commented. She paused, thinking again about how much she should relate to Jack. *What am I afraid of? I've already told him enough to let him know I'm in deep trouble.* Heidi looked into the eyes of the man sitting beside her. Jack's eyes filled with sympathy, with concern. She realized she could trust him. "My husband's name is Cain Lawson. The man who helped me escape is Lorenzo. He had a helper, Pete, who was the one who actually got me out of there. I fear, at this point, Cain might have figured out who helped me escape and that Lorenzo is dead."

"How do you know this?" Jack inquired.

"There was a murder this morning in Brantford. Pete contacted me and said Lorenzo had contacted him and needed to speak to him right away. Pete was going to see Lorenzo, but cops were all over his place. An ambulance was there, too, and they brought a body out of the house—in a body bag." Heidi choked the words out as quickly as she could, full of emotion. "It's all my fault. A good man lost his life because of me."

"Heidi, if you want me to, I can call my captain at the station and ask if they've identified the body yet. Maybe it isn't your friend, Lorenzo."

"I'd appreciate that, Jack … but, in reality, who else could it be?"

"We won't know until we have a name."

"Okay."

"Do you want to tell me anything more?" Jack asked, not wanting to force Heidi to talk further if she wasn't ready.

"I'd like to, but let me check on Alora first … and, could I get you a drink?"

"Glass of water would be good," Jack answered.

As Heidi disappeared into the house, Toby came over and jumped into Jack's lap. Jack stroked his friend's back. "Your hunch was right, old man. Heidi's in trouble and she's been too afraid to say anything until now. I wonder what kind of power this man, Cain, has that Heidi is so reluctant to turn him in. And, this guy, Lorenzo, why did he stick around so long? Why did he work for such a man, even after he knew what Cain did to his wife? Does Cain have something on him?" Jack rambled on with his thoughts.

Toby was doing some thinking of his own. Once again, he'd been spot on with feeling there was something wrong. And Toby knew even more than Jack. He knew there was a car casing Heidi's house. And the dog knew it too.

"I see your friend has joined us," Heidi commented as she handed Jack his glass of water. "Welcome, Toby," she added. Heidi sat down beside Jack and continued her story. "Lorenzo seemed concerned the first morning he returned to take me for a walk after witnessing my beating. I'd been confined to the house for a couple days. It was as though Lorenzo couldn't even look at me; my bruises were in full bloom. I finally got the courage to ask him if he would help me escape.

"Lorenzo was reluctant at first, and of course, he wouldn't commit to anything. Said he had to think about it. You can guess I feared I'd made a mistake. After all, Lorenzo was Cain's man, not mine. However, a few days later, he told me he would help, but I had to do what he said. He was formulating a plan and would let me know when he was ready to implement it. Until then, it was business as usual. The day came when Lorenzo told me he was leaving, and you can imagine how I felt. It was like a knife stabbing my heart. But Lorenzo told me it was all part of his plan. He'd handpicked his replacement to execute the plan. I was still afraid. I was comfortable with Lorenzo."

Heidi went on to tell Jack how Lorenzo was planning his exit. Jack remained silent and let her talk, absorbing each word. He thought what a scum Cain was. It never ceased to amaze Jack over the years he'd been in law enforcement how far some people would go to have power over others.

"I'm hungry, Mommy," Alora opened the door to the yard and squeezed in between her mom and Jack.

Toby jumped off Jack's lap, not in the mood to get pawed by the child. *Sorry, kid ... oh no, here comes the mutt too.* Toby decided he'd heard enough for one day. He knew Jack would rehash everything when he got home.

Jack stood and stretched his legs and glanced at his watch. "I think that might be enough for today," he said. "I'll come back in the morning if you like ... if you want to tell me more. In the meantime, I'll call my captain and try and find out who the victim was this morning."

Heidi stood and looked up at Jack. "I don't know what's going to happen here, Jack. If this goes bad, you might just want to step aside. There is one thing I want to ask you, though. If…" Heidi wasn't sure if she should go as far as to ask this next question, but with Lorenzo dead—probably—and Pete sort of in the wind, she needed to. "If Cain has found me and comes after me, I need to protect Alora…"

"Say no more," Jack declared quickly. "Your daughter will be safe with me."

"And, Bear?"

"Of course." Jack paused. "But let's hope it doesn't come down to that." Jack started to leave, then turned back. "Would you feel safer moving into my place? I have plenty of room."

Heidi swallowed hard. She couldn't believe her luck in having moved next door to such a kind man. And one who had substantial connections with the local police force. However, instead of accepting the invitation immediately, "Not right now … today … but it might be an option. Thank you." Heidi turned back into her house, guiding Alora ahead of her. Bear stayed outside.

From a distance, a man in a black car had a pair of binoculars focused on the backyard where Jack and Heidi were talking. When both parties went their separate ways, the man picked up his cell phone and dialled a number.

"We might have to move up the plan…"

22

Cain handed Cameron a set of keys to a black Cadillac. There was a sarcastic grin on Cain's face as he gave Cameron his last-minute warning. "Remember, Cameron—the keys are not a get-out-of-jail card. Your family will be safe as long as you're doing what I've sent you to do. Capisce?"

Cameron nodded. He took the proffered keys. However, before getting in the car, "What if I can't get the girl … what if your wife has her so guarded that I can't get near her?"

"Oh, I think you'll find a way," Cain emphasized with another unfriendly grin. "Your family's existence depends on your success. Your life depends on your bringing to me what is mine—my daughter." Cain stepped closer and jabbed a finger into Cameron's chest. "Don't let me down. I don't usually give people who have double-crossed me a second chance. Got it?"

Cameron nodded and tried to back away from Cain, whose breath reeked of alcohol. *The man is coming apart … drinks too much; I've never seen him sober since I've been here … might be my ticket out of this mess. But first, I have to get his kid for him and find out where my family is.*

Cain stepped back and gave his last-minute instructions. "There's an envelope in the glove box. Use the funds wisely to accomplish your task. You'll also find a cell phone there, which is programmed directly to my phone.

Just press “talk” and the number one. Let me know when you’ve got her and are on your way here.”

Cameron nodded again.

“One more thing,” Cain stepped forward and put his hand on the car door, preventing Cameron from getting in the vehicle. “If by chance you fail and get caught, remember that I have your family. It would be wise if you should feel inclined to tell the police about me or anything you’ve seen here, well, to think twice before speaking out. Do you understand ?”

Cameron nodded once more. His stomach was so tied up in knots he couldn’t speak to the man who had taken over his life—and that of his family.

“Good man,” Cain commented, giving Cameron a light slap on the cheek before backing away from the car and walking away.

Cameron got in the car and put the key in the ignition. He sat for a moment with his hands on the steering wheel, staring out the windshield. With a shuddering breath, Cameron finally turned the key and drove away from the hell he’d landed in towards what he knew was going to be another. The last thing Cameron wanted to do was kidnap an innocent kid, but the lives of his kids and wife depended on his success.

Cain watched the car leave, then turned and walked to his office. Mitch would be waiting for him, having called to say he had some vital information to relay and that he preferred to tell Cain in person. When Cain stepped into his office, Mitch was sitting in a chair in front of Cain’s desk, his feet resting on its corner.

"So, what do you have to tell me?" Cain got right to the point before opening a drawer and pulling out a mickey of scotch.

"Tomas is dead."

"What?"

"Yeah. Lorenzo must have seen Tomas coming and surprised him."

"Where's Lorenzo now?"

"In the wind." Mitch hesitated a moment, unsure if he should ask his question. Deciding he had nothing to lose, "Is the bitch worth all this, boss? After all, it's been two years, and she hasn't said anything to anyone yet." Another pause, then Mitch plunged forward. "I am thinking that stirring the pot like this might just tempt her to speak up."

Cain looked annoyed about what Mitch was suggesting. "Keep your thoughts to yourself about my family matters. I want my daughter, and I'll make it so my wife wouldn't dare say anything to anyone." Cain downed his glass of scotch. "Getting back to Lorenzo … I want you to get a couple of the guys—maybe Christoff and Markus––they've done some investigative work for me before. Have them put feelers out and report directly back to me when they find him."

"Do you want them to bring Lorenzo in?" Mitch questioned.

Cain scowled. "No. I just want to know where he is for now. Then I'm going to send him a little gift."

Mitch stood. "Well, I guess I better get going." Before leaving, though, "You want me to keep an eye on Cameron … make sure he's doing what he's supposed to?"

"Sure … good idea." Cain poured another drink and chugged it down even quicker than the first one. Mitch took the hint and left.

Cameron set the binoculars down on the seat beside him. Sweat broke out on his forehead and he could feel the moisture dripping from his armpits. He'd been watching the two individuals on the back stoop of the house for some time. He saw the little girl—Alora, Cain had told him his daughter's name—come out of the house, followed by a cat and a dog. *Cats are no problem, but a dog? It could present a real challenge for me, especially since I don't like dogs and they don't seem to like me much.*

The two adults stood. The man said something to the woman before he and the cat left and walked toward the house next door. *Good, the guy isn't part of the woman's life ... will make it easier to get to the child.*

Cameron watched Cain's wife and child make their way into their house; the dog stayed outside. Cameron decided to wait for another half-hour or so. It would be dark soon, and most likely the woman would be putting the kid to bed. Tomorrow was another day. After all, Cain hadn't given an exact deadline of when he was supposed to deliver his daughter.

23

Carrie was furious that Cameron had put the family in such a situation. The children, including stoic Colin, Cameron's son from his previous marriage, had cried themselves to sleep for two nights now. It wasn't that the accommodations weren't comfortable. It was that they were prisoners snatched from their beds in the middle of the night by some goons.

Cindy approached her mommy; her face was blotchy with tears. Carrie was chopping vegetables for supper. "How long do we have to stay here, Mommy? I want to go home. I miss my toys. I miss my bed. I miss my friends. I miss my daddy."

Carrie set the knife aside and knelt beside her daughter, gathering Cindy into her arms. "Oh, sweetie—just think of this as a little holiday. Daddy has some business to take care of, and then he'll be here to get us and take us home." Carrie hoped to give Cindy some hope, even though she didn't have much expectation that the situation was going to work out for the family.

Devlin came into the kitchen slowly. Ever since he'd come back from going with his dad and the man who had taken him, Devlin hadn't spoken a word. Carrie thought she was about to have a breakthrough with her son, but then men had come. The family was forced from their home and relocated to a place with window bars and outside locks on the doors. Devlin cuddled up to his mom and put his arms around her neck. Carrie stroked her son's hair and whispered in his ears that everything would be okay. He squeezed her harder.

Colin strode into the room and stood for a moment observing the scene in front of him. His stepbrother and stepsister annoyed him to no end. He'd been his father's only child until Carrie came into his father's life. What was happening now needed a strong character to deal with it, and if there was anything Colin was, it was tough. "I'll find a way, Carrie," Colin said as he walked to where the family was assembled. Colin never called Carrie "mom" despite his father telling him he should. "I'll get us out of here. I've been checking around, and I am sure this house has a weak spot that we can use to escape."

"Colin … I know you mean well, son," Carrie noticed how Colin tensed when she called him "son," but she continued talking, not caring. "But these men we are dealing with are not good people, and if we do anything to upset them, I have no idea what they will do to your dad. Despite what he did to put us in this position, I love him and will not be held responsible for anything bad that might happen to him." She paused before continuing to try and calm her stepson before he went any further. "Just lay low for now. I am sure this nightmare will be over before we know it. I know your dad will be doing everything humanly possible to get us free."

Carrie spoke the words but had no confidence in them. And from the look on Colin's face, she knew Cameron's son didn't have faith that things would work out for the better either. She also knew there was no way she would be able to stop this headstrong young boy from doing what he felt was the right thing to do!

A key turning in the lock of the back door leading into the kitchen caused Cindy to burst into tears and hide behind her mother. Devlin started to shake uncontrollably, and a wet spot appeared on the front of his sweatpants. Colin faced the door with more bravery than he was feeling.

The man who entered the kitchen was carrying four bags of groceries. He walked across to the table and set the bags down. “This should keep you for a few days,” he stated blandly. “I hope it’s to your liking,” he added. “Make a list for me for the next time I come if there’s anything special you want.” He pointed to one of the bags. “Better get that stuff in the freezer. I picked up some ice cream for the kids; I hope they like the flavour I got.”

Cindy and Devlin congregated behind their mother. “Colin, please take your brother and sister into the living room and turn the television on for them.” Carrie waited for the children to leave, noticing Colin wasn’t happy about it, despite obeying her. Once she was alone with the man, “How long does your boss intend to keep us here? And where is my husband? Why can’t I see him, or at least talk to him?”

“Look, lady. I got nothin’ to do with any of that. I’m just doin’ my job. You’ll have to ask the boss those questions if you want answers.”

“Well then, when is your boss going to present himself like a man and tell me why he’s doing this?”

“All I know, lady, is your husband has something to do for the boss, and maybe after he does the job, the boss’ll let you go. As I said, I’m just doin’ my job.” He walked to the door, turning at the last second, “Make the list if you need anything else. I’ll be back tomorrow night to pick it up.” With that, he left.

Carrie started going through the bags, laying the items out on the table, taking the things for the freezer and putting them away first. She had a sense she was being watched and looked nervously around the room, her eyes searching for a possible hidden camera.

From his office, Cain watched the computer screen, the one attached to the cameras in the house where he'd stashed Cameron's family. He leaned forward in his chair when he noticed that Carrie was looking around—from floor to ceiling.

"She's a smart one … thinking … but how would she know?" Cain muttered. He poured a shot of scotch and downed it in one gulp. "I'll have to watch her closely … and that boy, the oldest one. He's going to be trouble." Cain laughed. "Kid doesn't know that I'll know his every move before he makes it." Cain leaned in close to the computer screen. "No way out, little man. No way out. Not for your father … your mother … the two little brats. Definitely not for you, either."

Cain pushed his chair back and grinned as he grabbed his coat and set off out the door. He felt it was time to pay Cameron's family a little visit. Cain was too smart to house them near his place in the country; he found the family a secluded home in Brantford, close to where his wife, Jennifer, was living now. Cain laughed at the irony of what he was about to do—kidnap his daughter and place her in the care of Cameron's wife.

"I'm a bloody genius," Cain trilled as he got in his car.

24

Christoff and Markus received their orders to find Lorenzo as soon as possible. Markus, the bolder of the two men, was ready to dice Lorenzo into little pieces and feed the traitor to the pigs. Mitch told Markus that wouldn't be necessary; it wasn't what the boss wanted. They were to locate Lorenzo, and Cain would give further instructions from there. They weren't to touch Lorenzo in any way—yet.

Mitch drove off after talking to Christoff and Markus. He wanted to check out what Cameron was doing. Mitch parked down the street from where Jennifer lived and looked for the car Cain had lent to Cameron. "There you are, my friend. Good. You're on the job. Time for me to go and get a little R and R." Mitch started his car, pulled into a driveway, and turned the car to take off in the opposite direction of where Cameron was parked.

Heidi came downstairs from having tucked Alora into bed. She'd spent extra time with her daughter tonight, reading her two stories instead of one. Heidi wasn't sure what the next days were going to bring. She thought about what she had proposed to Jack—that Alora and Bear stay with him if she discovered for sure that Cain knew where she was. It was strange that she'd just met Jack but was willing to trust him impeccably with her daughter's life.

Bear whined at the back door to get out. "Okay ... okay." Heidi opened the doors for her dog. "There you go,

Bear. But remember, no barking." Bear took off into the yard, his tail wagging happily.

Heidi decided to sit on the stoop and watch her four-footed friend frolic in the grass. She leaned back against the wall of the house and closed her eyes. It was such a peaceful neighbourhood, not like the first two Lorenzo had found for her. Heidi wished she could go back to her former life, to the one where she was in control, where she had friends. *But one good thing came out of the nightmare—Alora. I wouldn't trade her for the world.*

An outside light went on in the yard behind Heidi's house, and a couple men walked onto its back porch. Heidi noticed them light cigarettes, and in the night atmosphere, she heard the snap of two beer cans opening. *I hope they aren't going to start partying at this time of night; people need to get their sleep.* Heidi stood and called to Bear to come in the house. Once inside, she filled the dog's dish with kibble; Bear was good with not overeating even when his bowl was full.

Heidi looked at her watch. As tired as she was, she didn't want to go to bed yet. She knew what to expect—a series of nightmares, Cain being front and centre on their stage. Heidi walked into the living room, folded herself into a corner of the couch, and turned on the television. She flicked through the channels looking for something of interest, finally leaving it on a news station. *Maybe there'll be something about Lorenzo.* Heidi pulled a couch-throw up and wrapped it around her. Within minutes though, she was fast asleep.

Jack was true to his word. As soon as he left Heidi, he called Captain Wagner at the Brantford police station. "Hey, Bryce. I need a favour if it is possible for you to grant it."

"What's up, Jack? You know I'll help you if I can."

"Has the name of this morning's victim from the homicide on Dufferin Ave been released yet?"

"Let me check for you, Jack … I'll get right back to you. I believe the officers who were at the scene just finished the paperwork."

"Thanks, Bryce."

Jack busied himself in the kitchen while he waited, preparing a light supper. He looked around, wondering where Toby was. It wasn't typical for the old cat to not be home at this time of night—supper time! Jack went to the backdoor and opened it. He looked around to see if Toby was nearby. Nowhere to be seen. Jack stepped back into the house and closed the door.

"He'll come home when he's ready," Jack said to the empty room, then went about finishing his supper preparation.

As Jack sat down to eat, his phone rang. He checked the caller I.D. and saw it was the captain. "Bryce," Jack said. "Thanks for getting back to me so quickly. Did you discover the name for me?"

"Yes. Our victim is a small-time crook by the name of Tomas Abila."

Hmmm … not Heidi's Lorenzo … I wonder about the connection.

"You still there, Jack?" Captain Bryce broke the temporary silence. "Is that all you needed?"

"If there's anything else you can tell me, I'd appreciate it."

"Let me ask first, what is your interest in this case?"

"I'd rather not say at the moment … please trust me on this and give me some leeway."

"Okay. We don't have a suspect yet—well, not a name, anyway. It wasn't Abila's apartment. The neighbours said an older man was living there, but he kept pretty much to himself, and no one knew his name. Word indicated the guy hadn't lived there that long. The police found two bullet casings in the mattress of the room where the victim was—obviously not the bullets that killed Abila. He was killed with two bullets right to the heart, still in his body."

"So, what you are saying is the tenant might have been expecting someone to come and try to kill him and was ready."

"Best scenario, as I see it from here."

"Thank you, Bryce … I owe you one."

Bryce laughed. "We lost count, didn't we, of who owes who over the years."

Jack chuckled. "You're right on that one."

After hanging up the phone, Jack thought of calling Heidi and telling her the good news, that the victim was not her friend, Lorenzo, and it appeared he had escaped. Jack looked at his watch and decided to wait until morning. Nothing could be done at this late hour, anyway.

Toby watched the two cars from his perch on the back of the couch, wondering why two vehicles were watching Heidi's place now. Toby decided to move closer. When he left, Jack was snoozing. He made his way down the street toward the furthest parked car, keeping close to the bushes. *One can't be too cautious. Whoever has been watching might also have seen me, and I am not a figure easily forgotten.* Toby was right across the street from the black limo, so he settled down by a thick bush. *Interesting, how the guy in the car only seems engrossed in the vehicle that is parked closer to Heidi's.*

Time ticked by slowly, and Toby had almost dozed off when he heard the limo start. He managed to hide just before the vehicle pulled into the lane of the house Toby was sitting by. Toby circled over to a maple tree, which was large enough to conceal him. He got a good cat's-eye view of the man in the car, searing his face into his mind. Once the car took off down the street, Toby made his way back to Heidi's and sat by her steps, watching the man in the Cadillac. The man watched the house with a set of binoculars. Eventually, that car took off, as well. Toby made his way home.

I doubt anything else is going to happen tonight. May as well get some sleep. I have a feeling I might need it…

Cain pulled into the driveway of the house where he was keeping Cameron's family. He knew no one would see him walking up to the house because the window coverings were drawn securely in place. Cain slipped his key into the lock and stepped inside. He could hear the television playing in the living room. Cain tiptoed to the entrance of where the family was sitting. Their mother was cuddling the two little ones on the couch; the oldest child sat alone in a chair beside the sofa. Cain stood a moment in the doorway.

"Well, well, well," Cain mocked the little group. "What a pleasant scene we have here."

Carrie pulled her children closer, if that was possible, as they were already pushing themselves behind her. "Who are you?" Carrie demanded, despite the butterflies attacking her stomach.

"Who am I?" Cain walked further into the room and took a seat across from the couch. "I am the man that holds your life in my hands."

Cindy began crying, and Devlin peed himself.

Carrie swallowed hard, digging for courage. "What do you want with us? How long do you expect you will be able to keep us here without someone finding out?"

Cain liked the woman's spunk. He wished Jennifer had been like that; it would have made his game more fun. "No one will find you, my dear," Cain replied with a sneer. "This house has been here for years, just as it is. Well hidden behind a tall cedar hedge. As for what I want from you … well, nothing in particular from you directly. Your husband tried to take something from me that wasn't his to take. I could have eliminated my problem, but when I learned he had such a beautiful family, I had a change of heart."

"Do you call this a change of heart? Terrifying young children. Taking them from their home in the dark of night, hands tied behind their backs and blindfolds over their eyes? Driving around for hours in the back of a van, laying on a cold, steel floor!" Carrie interrupted the intruder, angrily spewing forth a torrent of words.

"I am sure you prefer this to what I could have done to you and your husband," Cain retorted. "Your husband is alive, my dear. You are alive." Cain waved a hand toward the children. "Your brats are alive."

"For how long?" Carrie demanded.

"Now, that's a good question." Cain hesitated, then a slow smile crept across his face. "That is totally up to your husband, and how well he performs the task that I have given him."

Carrie wasn't about to give up questioning the man. "Why are you here now? What is the purpose of your visit? Did you just want to see how you have terrified my children?"

"Something like that." Cain stood, deciding he'd had enough of this woman's questions. She was becoming tiresome. "Well, I'll be off. I hope everything here is to your liking. My men will keep you supplied with whatever you need."

Carrie was about to reply with a smart crack but decided against it. She realized there was no use trying to get through to the man; he was colder than ice.

Cain stopped in the living room doorway, turned, and gave Carrie a strange look. "I will see you again, Carrie. Next time I might stay a little longer, and we can have a private chat—without the brats around." Cain's eyes swept hungrily over Carrie's body. *I'd love a piece of that … I'd show her what a real man is … not like the wimp she married.* Cain departed with a soft chuckle.

Carrie heard the threat in Cain's voice. She sat frozen on the couch, her arms around her two younger children. Even Colin cuddled closer to his step-mother, feeling the evil in the man who had visited the family.

25

The next morning promised rain. Dark clouds moved angrily across the sky, attempting to chase away the sun. Heidi couldn't help the feeling of desolation that encompassed her. She felt she was doomed no matter what she did, and was still trying to fathom how she'd ended up in this situation. Heidi wondered if Jack found out the name of the victim in yesterday's homicide.

Getting out of bed, she made her way to the bathroom. She heard the television downstairs. *Alora must be up early.* Hiedi glanced at her watch and realized she'd overslept. Quickly, she finished up in the bathroom, got dressed, and went downstairs. Bear greeted her in the kitchen when he heard her approach.

"Morning, Bear," Heidi said.

Bear's tail wagged furiously as he tried to jump up on his mistress.

"Down, Bear," Heidi gently pushed the dog away. She went to the door and opened it for Bear to go outside. "Out you go," she smiled.

Bear darted out the door and into the yard. Heidi stood for a moment, watching the dog as he went about his business. Bear was a beautiful dog, but Heidi had misgivings about how much he would protect her and Alora. Samoyeds were more known for how friendly they were, not for being great guard dogs. Heidi knew Bear wouldn't stay outside for long; the rain was starting. She made her way to the living room to say good morning to her daughter.

Toby woke early. He'd spent the night on the back of the couch, giving up the comfort of the end of Jack's bed. Toby was worried. He felt something big was going to go down, and it was going to happen sooner than later. The house was still quiet and didn't smell like morning yet. That meant Jack was still sleeping.

Can't sleep in, Jack. We need to be vigilant. Too many strange cars are hanging around here … checking out Emma's … I mean, Heidi's place … I got a good look at one of them, though … looks like a tough guy … he was watching the other guy who was watching Heidi's house … come on, Jack … time you got up … we have work to do. Toby made his way down the hallway and into Jack's bedroom. He jumped up on the bed and began to circle on Jack's pillow, letting out a couple of sharp meows.

Jack rolled over, slowly opening his eyes. He glanced at his window and saw the light peeking through the sides of the curtains. He groaned and shoved the covers off. "Okay, old man. Guess you're right … it's time to get the day going." As Jack was making his way to the bathroom, he heard the phone ring. "Wonder who that can be," he grumbled, taking a detour from his destination and heading to the living room to answer the phone.

"Hello," Jack barked into the receiver.

A chuckle came over the line. "Too early to call you, Jack?" Captain Wagner gave Jack a moment to realize who was calling so early in the morning. Then, "I have a bit of new information for you about our homicide yesterday, if you have a second."

Jack perked up, ready to listen. "Give me a minute to grab a pen and paper; go ahead … appreciate this, Bryce."

"One of our officers contacted the owner of the house to see if we could get the name of the gentleman who lived in the upper apartment. The owner returned our call last night and told us the name of the tenant was Lorenzo Marino—said he paid cash upfront for three months."

Jack finished writing down Lorenzo's name. "I can't thank you enough for this, Bryce. If anything else comes up, I'd appreciate it."

"No problem, Jack … you know, I don't know what's going on over in your neck of the woods, but be careful. I ran background checks on Tomas and Lorenzo; they aren't the cleanest guys in the book. Their past is shady, and from what's going down here, not so much in the past." A pause. "You know where we are if you need us." The captain hung up the phone, not waiting for another thank you from his old friend.

Jack left the slip of paper beside the phone and returned to his morning wake-up routine. He'd call Heidi right after breakfast.

Lorenzo was nervous. He knew Cain well enough that if his old boss had figured out his role in the disappearance of his wife, there would be more men coming after him. All Lorenzo could do was pray that the location he found would be off the grid. But he also knew Cain's resources were limitless. Lorenzo figured Cain would call in a couple of his enforcers—Christoff and Markus. They'd done several clean-up jobs for Cain in the past.

But I know you guys … I know how you work. Can't fool an old dog like me; I been around a long time, and I ain't alive because I was careless.

Lorenzo opened up his tablet and typed in his password. When the screen came up, he went directly to the program that would show him the perimeter of the property, where he'd implanted several cameras. Everything looked quiet. Lorenzo turned the tablet off and retrieved his gym bag. Digging around, Lorenzo pulled out a bag, which housed some items that would disguise his looks. By the time Lorenzo left the cabin, even his mother wouldn't have recognized him.

As he drove out the laneway and onto the side road, Lorenzo punched the number for Pete's phone into his cell. Pete answered after six rings.

"We need to meet," Lorenzo wasted no time getting to the point. "Where are you at the moment?"

"At the Holiday Inn Express on Sinclair Blvd … building one," Pete replied.

"Too public," Lorenzo replied quickly. He thought for a moment of some of the locations he'd already scoped out. "There's a group of homeless people camped out behind the old police station on Greenwich Street. Get yourself together and meet me there in half an hour."

"I assume you are in disguise?"

"You assume correctly. And, if I were you, I'd make sure you do a little something to camouflage who you are, as well. I'll be the bum wearing a large green-checkered lumber jacket. See you in half an hour. Oh, and make sure no one follows you. I have a feeling Cain will have sent out a couple of his enforcers to track not only me but you, especially now that you haven't returned to the base."

"I don't like this one bit, Lorenzo. You got a soft spot for a dame and landed us in a bad situation…"

Lorenzo cut his friend off: "You agreed to this, Pete. I think we need to get Heidi and her daughter out of the country—only way we're going to be able to keep them alive. Get here, and I'll discuss my plan with you." Lorenzo hung up.

The drive into Brantford didn't take Lorenzo long, but his eyes were continuously scanning his car mirrors and out his windows. He took the BSAR and turned onto Greenwich from there. Lorenzo drove past the old police station and parked his car at an animal hospital just down and across the street. He locked the vehicle and walked to the other side of the road. A couple teenagers passed on the sidewalk and told the bum they saw to get a life. Lorenzo held his temper and continued on his way, staggering for effect until he was out of sight behind the station.

What Lorenzo saw there made his heart bleed. *People shouldn't have to live like this, not in a country so rich. We send money to other countries for their homeless––what about our own?* Lorenzo stopped by a large oak tree and sat down on the ground, his back leaning on the trunk.

Ten minutes after his arrival, Lorenzo noticed Pete coming across the park. *Good man, Pete … just a couple of bums meeting up in a park.* Lorenzo remained on the ground. Pete knelt beside him.

"Were you followed?" Lorenzo looked beyond Pete.

"Not that I know of."

"Good … okay … let's take a walk. Make sure you limp like the old man you're dressed as." Lorenzo half-smiled.

As the two men walked, Lorenzo told Pete what the plan was and what his part in it would be. "I want you to fill Heidi in on this and give her the instructions to prepare to move on a minute's notice—most likely by the end of the week."

"What about the dog?"

"Bear has to be left behind this time." Lorenzo knew that might cause a problem, but there was no other way. He thought he might be able to buy some time by having Bear visible in the yard where Heidi was currently staying. "I'll be in touch later to confirm that you've spoken to Heidi and to get her response," Lorenzo added. "Be careful ... we are far from out of danger."

26

Jack decided to go directly to Heidi's place and tell her what he'd found out. Toby didn't come with him, which he found strange, but then again, Toby was a peculiar cat. Jack and Heidi sat at the kitchen table, and after Jack relayed his information, he could tell Heidi could barely contain her joy when Jack told her Lorenzo was still alive.

"At least I think he is," Jack added. "We have no proof. The man seems to have disappeared."

"Lorenzo knows what he's doing," Heidi said. "He's careful beyond being careful. I will probably hear from Pete before long with directions on what I am to do." Heidi hesitated. She was still unsure about what she was going to do. She was tired of running. Lorenzo would want her to run again, but this time for an even better reason. This time, it appeared Cain knew where she was. She had a sinking feeling she may be leaving her country's shores behind her.

"Where's Alora?" Jack asked, getting a sudden weird feeling in his gut.

"She wanted to play on the front porch. Alora loves watching the rain, and..." Suddenly, Heidi's face turned white. "Oh, my God! Alora!"

Heidi and Jack raced to the front of the house, throwing open the front door and stepping out onto the porch. "Alora!" Heidi screamed when she didn't see her child. "Oh, God! Oh, God!" She turned to Jack and fell into his arms, sobbing hysterically. "She's gone, Jack! Cain's got her!"

Toby's reason for not going with Jack was so he could keep an eye on Alora. From his perch on the back of the couch, the cat noticed Alora playing on the front porch. *What's Heidi thinking, letting the kid play that close to the street? And where's the mutt?—probably chasing squirrels in the backyard. I better keep my eye on things. God, I hate this rain.* Toby squeezed out his cat-door and made his way to a spot at the side of the porch, hiding under a bush.

Moments after Toby settled under the foliage, he heard a car engine approaching. As the car slowed down, Toby saw it was one of the vehicles that had been on the street the night before. The car stopped. A man got out and moved quickly to the porch where Alora was playing. Toby's heart went into overdrive. *Shit! It's going down; what can I do to stop this—I gotta do something! Oh, look, the guy left his door open … if I can get in the car and hide, at least I'll know where he's taking the kid. Then, I'll come back and get help … these bad guys don't know who they're dealing with—Detective Toby is on the job!*

As Cameron was chloroforming Alora, Toby raced across the sidewalk and into the car. He jumped over the front seat and burrowed under a blanket on the floor in the back, just in time before Cameron opened the vehicle's back door and put Alora on the seat. Hurriedly, he raced to the driver's seat, got in, and without even putting his seatbelt on, stepped on the gas and raced down the street. Cameron slowed down at the four-way stop but went right on through the intersection when he saw it was clear. Finally, after driving several blocks. Cameron pulled over and parked, and took out the cell phone Cain had given him.

“Cameron,” Cain’s voice came over the line. “I hope you have good news for me. Do you have my daughter?”

Cameron’s voice was shaky as he provided the answer Cain was waiting for. “Yes.”

“Good job. Okay, this is what you’re going to do now. There will be a car waiting for you at the Holiday Inn Express on Sinclair Blvd; do you know where that is?”

“Yeah.”

“Good. When you get there, you will get out of your car and wait for the driver of the other vehicle to approach you. He will hand you the keys to his car and will take yours. They will be taking my daughter to her final destination.”

“She’s not coming out to your place?” Cameron questioned curiously, thinking this was a strange turn of events.

“It’s none of your business where I am taking my daughter,” Cain snapped. “Now, once you get into the other car, look in the glove compartment for an envelope, which holds your next set of instructions.”

“I thought all I had to do was get you your kid!” Cameron was angry at the turn of events. “When do I get to see my family? When are you going to let us go?”

“Do you think, Cameron, by doing me one little job, you’ve paid your debt? You are a fool, aren’t you? I’ll tell you when I’m done with you. Now, you have a meeting to go to. We’ll talk soon.” Cain hung up the phone.

Cameron sat behind the wheel for a few more minutes, then finally put the car in drive and pulled out into the traffic. Toby had only heard one half of the conversation, but what he’d heard was not good. Alora was still asleep on the backseat. As Cameron turned onto the street leading to the Holiday Inn, he didn't see Pete's car turning out of the hotel's driveway.

The car came to another stop, and Toby's heart beat faster than usual. *What now? The guy is getting out … are we at the location of the drop-off … hope I can find my way home to get help. Wait … I hear footsteps approaching … jeez … I wish I could get out from under this blanket and see what's going on.*

"That's the kid?" A new voice asked.

"Yes," Cameron replied.

"Okay. Here are the keys to that black car parked at the end of the last row over there. I assume the boss gave you your orders?"

"Yeah, I got my orders," Cameron confirmed sarcastically.

"Good."

Toby felt the car shake as the person got into the driver's seat. *Must be a big guy—car is tilting.* The automobile moved on. Toby relaxed. All he could do now was wait and see where the end of the journey would be. From the length of time the vehicle travelled, Toby felt they were heading back to where he lived. Of course, the cat had no idea what direction they were moving in, so it was foolish even to think along that line. After a short length of time, the car slowed down, and it seemed to Toby that it was turning into a driveway. The driver put the vehicle in park, got out and came around to the back door. As he reached in to get Alora, Toby got a good look at him. *Yep, this guy should be on a diet.* Toby watched for his chance to leap out of the car.

The man struggled for a moment to lift Alora off the seat. When he finally had her secure in his arms, he stepped back and moved away from the car. *How lucky can a cat get? The guy's left the door open for me!* Toby darted out of the car and raced to the cedar hedge surrounding the house where the man was taking Alora.

Toby slunk as close as possible without being noticed by the man, who was on the step, fumbling in his pocket for keys. Juggling the dead-weight child to one side, the man opened the door and stepped inside the house. Toby came out from the bushes and padded up the sidewalk, giving the house a good look. All the windows were heavily covered. Toby looked out at the street.

This place looks familiar … I think I've seen it before. Toby made his way down to the sidewalk, and there was a park that looked like the one near Jack's house. But it wasn't the same one; the play area had different equipment. *Well, here goes … I need to follow the streets in the area up and down …look for and remember land sights so I can trace my way back here with help.*

Toby turned and took a good look at the house. Of course, the most obvious thing about the house was the tall cedar hedge surrounding it, something none of the other homes on the street within Toby's line of sight had. Toby set off, hoping to reach home quickly so he could get someone back to save little Alora, and whoever else might be imprisoned in that house!

27

Carrie, who was in the kitchen washing dishes, was stunned by the intrusion. Colin, Devlin, and Cindy were in the living room watching cartoons. "What the…" Carrie dropped the plate she was drying; it smashed on the tile floor.

The man didn't smile as he spoke. "Where's a place I can put this kid?" he grumbled, as though Alora was too heavy for him.

Instead of answering the man's question, Carrie pummelled him with questions. "Who are you? And who is this child? What's going on here?"

"Look, lady. Let me put the kid down, and then I'll explain everything to you."

Carrie pursed her lips, set her towel on the counter, and sidestepped around the broken dish. "Follow me."

With Alora tucked under a blanket on the bed in Cindy's room, Carrie and the intruder returned to the kitchen. "Give me a minute to clean up this mess," Carrie said, grabbing a broom from a closet in the corner of the kitchen.

The man sat down at the table and folded his hands on the table. Carrie noticed he seemed unhappy about what he was doing. *You have a choice, mister. If you are involved with that man—Cain—the same man who has my husband doing his will … who is holding my children and me as hostages … you are free to get out. Maybe even help me to get out.* Carrie swept the broken plate into a dustpan and dumped the pieces into the garbage, then sat down at the table opposite the man. She kept her hands folded on her lap, out of sight, not wanting the intruder to see how nervous she was.

"Is everything okay, Carrie?" Colin showed up in the doorway. "I heard … oh, we have company."

Carrie turned and looked at her stepson, giving him a stern look. "Everything is fine, Colin. Go back to the living room and look after Cindy and Devlin. Stay with them until I finish here."

Colin hesitated. Finally, he turned and left, but not before throwing an angry look at the man in the kitchen.

"So, what's the deal here, mister?" Carrie asked.

"The kid's name is Alora. She's Cain's daughter. Cain's wife took the girl and disappeared with her a couple years ago. He recently discovered where they were, and is just retrieving his property."

"Property!" Carrie spits angrily. "A child is not property! And, from what I know of your boss, from personal experience," Carrie waved her hand around the room, pointing to the locked door and the window coverings that couldn't open, "I think the woman—Cain's wife—must have had good reason to run and hide."

The man cleared his throat. Carrie could tell he was a smoker by the rasping sound of his words. "Ain't my business, lady. I got orders to pick up the kid and bring her here. You'll look after her until the boss comes for her. Capisco?" The man stood and put his fists on the table. He leaned over and looked Carrie directly in the eyes. "By the way, your husband did a great job of procuring the kid for Cain. Which is a good thing for you, I'd say, because he's passed the first loyalty test." The man started toward the door after dropping his bombshell on Carrie. Just before leaving, "I'll be back tomorrow with some more supplies for you; anything you need besides the basics?"

"A key to open the door!" Carrie huffed.

The man laughed on his way out. The lock clicked into place.

A shriek resounded throughout the house, turning into a wail. Carrie jumped up from the table and raced down the hallway to Cindy's room. The little girl was sitting up in the bed, hysterical, her eyes wide with terror. Alora shrunk back into the covers when Carrie entered the room. "Where's my mommy?" she blubbered. "Where am I?" I want my mommy!" The sobbing wouldn't stop.

Carrie was beside herself what to do. She had no idea, other than a name, who this child was. Slowly, she walked toward the bed. "It's okay, Alora … the man who brought you here told me your name…"

"Are you a bad lady … where's Mommy … I want my mommy!"

Carrie stood beside the bed but didn't reach out to the child. She knew there was a need to build some sort of rapport—if possible—to get the child to trust her. " Alora, I am not a bad lady. I am here in this house the same way you are. Someone brought me here against my will—my children and me. As for your mommy, I assume she is at home missing you terribly, but I don't know where your home is. I don't even know where we are. I was blindfolded when the people took me from my house."

Alora listened carefully to what Carrie was saying, and her sobs began to lessen. "Did that bad man bring you here?"

"Not the one who brought you … different ones." Carrie dared to sit on the edge of the bed. Alora cringed but didn't try to move further away. "Would you like to meet my children? I have a little girl who looks to be about your age. Are you five?"

Alora nodded.

Carrie heard a noise in the doorway. She turned and saw her three children standing there, staring at the stranger in Cindy's bed. Carrie motioned for the kids to step in closer. "Children, this is Alora. She will be staying with us for a while until her father comes for her."

Alora started to shake. "My daddy's a bad man. He's mean. I don't want to see him. Mommy ran away from him. Uncle Lorenzo and Uncle Pete helped her. They helped Mommy and me and Bear to get away from Daddy." Alora resumed crying, clenching her little hands into fists and hitting herself on the legs. "Don't let my daddy take me away, please."

Carrie wasn't sure how to handle the situation. She knew she had no control over what happened to Alora; she had no control over what happened to her children, or herself. She looked at Alora, her eyes filled with sympathy. *Oh, you poor, dear child, how can I help you? What your mother must be going through right now, I can only imagine. Cain is a monster for what he's doing to his child, and probably for what he's already done in the past to elicit such terror.*

Cindy stepped further into the room and walked over to a toy box sitting in a corner. She dug around until she came up with a Raggedy-Ann doll, then walked over to Alora and handed it to her. Carrie watched as the two little girls made eye contact. "I call my doll Annie," Cindy said. "She helps me when I'm feeling sad."

Alora stopped crying and reached for the doll, hugging it close to her chest and burying her face in the mop-top curls. The two little girls were having a moment, and Alora seemed calm with Cindy there, so Carrie backed slowly out of the room and motioned for the boys to follow her. When she returned a half an hour later, both girls where curled up on the bed sleeping with their arms around each other.

28

Cain was waiting impatiently for the phone call that would inform him his daughter's kidnapping was successful. When it finally came, he sat down in his chair and smiled. "I'll teach you to cross me, you bitch!" Cain picked up the picture of himself and Jennifer on their wedding day. He had to admit, she was beautiful. It had been challenging to control his dark side when he'd first met Jennifer in Cuba, but she was a damsel in distress, and he'd been looking for a woman he could use to promote himself up the ladder of his business dealings. When he saw her that day on the beach, his first thought was that she'd make a lovely trophy-wife on his arm.

However, Jennifer had proven not to be such a submissive little woman. She hadn't wanted to leave her job and just look after his needs. And Cain was a needy man. He controlled those needs for so long, but then couldn't stand it any longer and began taking more and more business trips. He'd managed to convince Jennifer to move to the country, telling her it would be a great place to raise a family when they decided it was time to start one. She'd mentioned she wanted kids. He didn't but thought that eventually, they'd add to his image of being a family man. After Alora was born, Jennifer became consistently problematic, and Cain had no choice but to lock her up. She asked too many questions and was seeing too much of his operation since moving to the country property.

A knock on his office door brought Cain out of his daydreaming. “Come in,” he barked.

Cameron entered but stayed close to the doorway. He’d been shocked when he’d read the instructions Cain had given him. There was no way Cameron wanted anything more to do with this man.

“Why are you here?” Cain sneered. “Aren’t you supposed to be collecting something for me from the names on the list I gave you?”

Cameron nodded. “Here’s the thing … I went to the first place, and an older man answered the door. He wasn’t on the list, but his son, sitting at the table stoned out of his mind, was. I asked him if he had your money, and the kid started to cry. The older man begged me to leave them alone—said he would get me the money, but I had to give him time to go to the bank and arrange for a loan. Then he asked me how much his son owed, and when I told him, the father’s face paled. I knew right then that he couldn’t raise so much money.

“I walked over to the kid and told him he was a piece of shit—a piece of shit just like me. I told him that I tried to cross you, and now I was paying dearly for it. I even made a pretence of going to rough the kid up, but the father stepped in and begged me not to hurt his son … told me the kid was all he had, and despite him not being a shining example of humankind, the boy was all he had. I wasn’t willing to beat the kid in front of the old man—just couldn’t do it.” Cameron shifted uncomfortably, realizing the man in front of him didn’t care one iota about the old man, the kid, or anyone else for that matter, other than himself.

Cain was watching Cameron closely. He was annoyed this man he’d given another chance to was making decisions that would affect him. Cain watched as Cameron squirmed with discomfort, and at that point, Cain knew he had the man in the palm of his hand and was now going to make him pay for what he'd done—hadn't done! Cain stood and walked over to where Cameron was standing.

"Do you realize what you have done here?" Cain began. "I was going to let you talk to your family when I heard what a great job you did of getting my daughter for me. But you couldn't let well enough alone, could you?" A pause.

Cameron opened his mouth to speak, but Cain raised a finger. "Don't … you've lost your right to speak at the moment. Do as I tell you—nothing more. You're not to think outside the box I have put you in, or you just may end up in a different sort of box—one more fitting for a sombre occasion. One that will line up nicely with … let me see…" Cain raised his hand and slowly released four fingers, "will line up with four similar boxes. How does that sound to you, Cameron? Would you like to see that? Oh, did I forget to mention something? Before you go into your box, I will have the pleasure of showing you what is in the other four boxes."

Cain took great satisfaction as he saw Cameron's face drain of colour. Cain was pleased with the effect his words had on this man. "So, what do you say, Cameron? Are you ever going to go outside my box again?"

Cameron couldn't bring himself to speak at the moment. The threat, not to his life, but to his family, was more than he could bear.

"Speak up, man!" Cain shouted testily. He was getting bored with the conversation. He had more important things to do other than handle a wimp that he should have just eliminated in the first place. *I shouldn't have taken pity on you … sucker for a pretty face … and your wife has a lovely look … some other pretty attractive parts to her, too,*

I bet! "Well … I'm waiting for your answer; are you going to be a good boy now, Cameron?"

Cameron finally found his voice. "Yeah."

Cain reached out and slapped Cameron's face, three firm taps. "Good. Now, get back to work. Get me what I asked for. Complete the entire list. I don't want to see your face until then. Capisce?"

Cameron nodded. His hatred for Cain was boiling in his gut, and Cameron didn't trust himself to open his mouth and speak. He feared the loathing for Cain might ring through in his words.

When Cameron didn't move immediately: "Get out of here. Finish your job, and then I'll think about letting you see your family." Cain turned and walked back to his desk, dismissing Cameron.

Cameron threw a look of pure contempt at Cain's back, then about-faced to the car. As he drove away, Cameron tried to think of a way out of his nightmare.

29

Jack gathered Heidi into his arms, trying desperately to calm her down. He knew, under the circumstances, there would be no right way of doing that. The man Heidi had described was a monster. Finally, Heidi pushed away. The resolute look on her face told Jack the young woman was a fighter. He reached into his pocket and pulled out his cell phone.

"I'm going to call my contact at the station and get the police on this immediately," he informed Heidi.

Bryce answered on the sixth ring, out of breath. "Wagner, here."

"Bryce … Jack, here. We have a big problem. You know the information I asked you for—it was for my neighbour. Well, things have gone south; someone kidnapped her daughter."

"Jack, are you telling me the two cases are connected?"

"Very connected. I need you to get a police crew out here and go over the area to see if we can pick up any clues as to who the abductor might be. A little girl … five years old … has been torn from her home and is God knows where."

"I'll get a cruiser there immediately," Bryce declared. "Are you with your neighbour now?"

"Yes. I'll not leave her at the moment."

"Good. See you soon."

Jack turned to Heidi, who was watching him with eyes red with grief. “The police are on their way,” he stated.

Heidi whispered, “Thank you.”

Bear was at the door, whining to come in. Heidi strolled to the door, and when the dog entered the room, Heidi crumbled to the floor. Bear moved directly into her arms and allowed his mistress to pour another flood of tears into his fur. Jack stood back, allowing Heidi her moment with Bear, his own heart breaking to pieces. Jack never had children of his own, but he’d dealt with numerous people throughout his police career who’d been traumatized by the loss of their children.

Jack was also beginning to wonder where Toby was. He hadn’t seen the old cat in the morning, which was strange for Toby to leave before eating. *Maybe there was enough leftover kibble in the dish from the evening snack to satisfy Toby’s morning appetite.* Jack wandered into the living room and watched out the front window for the police to arrive. It was still raining, although it had let up some and was just coming down in a drizzle now.

A few minutes later, Captain Bryce Wagner’s cruiser pulled up and parked in front of the house, followed by another police car. Jack greeted Bryce at the door. “Thanks for getting here so quickly, Bryce,” Jack said, letting the captain into the house.

Bryce got right down to business. “Where’s the mother?”

“In the kitchen,” Jack replied, leading the way.

Jack and Bryce didn’t have to go to the kitchen; Heidi appeared in the entrance. Jack made the introductions, and Bryce took over from there. Bryce motioned to Jack to let the two officers that were waiting on the porch into the house. He wanted to get an idea of precisely what had taken place before he set his people to work. Then, Bryce turned to Heidi and took out a notepad and pen.

"I need to ask you a few questions, Heidi, and please, don't take offence if you don't like my question … anything I ask is necessary. Do you understand?"

Heidi nodded, dreading she was going to have to repeat her story, so soon after relating it to Jack. Bryce went over everything, going right back to the beginning of how Heidi had met Cain. The captain had done some research before coming over and had discovered Cain Lawson was not an upright citizen. However, he'd never done jail time, or even been arrested, had been under surveillance on numerous occasions. People that had worked for Cain had served time, though, mostly for drug trafficking, but not one of them had ever turned on the man.

Finally, when he'd asked all his questions, Bryce turned to the two officers who had remained standing by the door. "Go over the porch with a fine-tooth comb, and the walkway leading up to the house. I also want you to check the other side of the street—go down about four or five houses on each side. If there's a cigarette butt … pop can … anything on the ground, I want it bagged and sent for testing. Whoever took Alora has probably been watching the house, waiting for their chance when she would be alone without her mother or the dog."

The officers left the house and got to work. Bryce picked up his phone and called the station, asking for more officers to come out and help comb the area. He also instructed the dispatcher to put out a red-alert for Alora, describing the child in detail from a picture Heidi handed him. When he got off the phone, Bryce turned to Heidi again: "I'd like to see the contents of the box you are keeping upstairs. We may be able to find a clue as to who your husband might have used to kidnap your daughter."

Heidi nodded and went upstairs, returning a few minutes later with the box. She handed it to Bryce, then returned to her spot on the couch. Bear pushed his way to his mistress and laid his head on her leg. Absently, Heidi stroked her dog's head. Her heart was breaking inside; her head was about to explode. She prayed this would be the end—that Cain would finally pay for how he'd ruined her life. She prayed that Alora would be okay.

Toby made his way down to the first stop sign. He stopped and looked both ways, trying to decide which direction to go. *Thank goodness the heavy rain has stopped. As it is, I'm probably going to catch pneumonia from getting so wet this morning … shouldn't have gotten involved … if Jack had just stayed home and not bothered with the new neighbour, I'd not be sitting at this stop sign, soaked through to my skin.* Toby decided to turn left.

After walking along for about twenty minutes, Toby realized he was heading in the direction of downtown. *Damn! I'll have to backtrack now and go the other way. I wish I'd eaten a bit more, but then I might have missed that guy who kidnapped the kid. Thing is, the guy switched places with that big fellow … more than one person involved here … wonder why. What's the point of kidnapping Alora and bringing her here, if the one who stole her was her father? Why not just take her to his house—why the switch? So, it wasn't her father … and the big guy? … definitely not the father.* Toby kept trying to figure out what was going on as he made his way back to the stop sign.

By the time he reached his destination, the rain had almost stopped. Toby looked back in the direction of the house with the tall cedar fence, wondering if he should maybe walk back there and check things out. Deciding that might be a good idea, Toby returned to the house. When he got there, he walked around to the backyard. Everything seemed sealed up as tight as a drum. From inside the house, Toby thought he could hear a child crying.

Toby started to circle the perimeter of the house, searching for a spot that he might be able to jump up on a windowsill. Nothing. Toby gazed up at the windows. All fully covered. Not a crack to be able to get a look through, even if he could find a way up to a sill. Feeling he'd thoroughly checked out the possibility of any way into the house, Toby made his way back to the street, and down to the stop sign. This time he turned right.

Captain Wagner poured through the papers and pictures Heidi had in the box. He laid them out on the coffee table and began to shuffle the photos around, putting them in different orders until he was satisfied with the layout.

Jack came and sat down beside Bryce. "Looks like you recognize some of the guys in these pictures," he commented.

"I do." Bryce pointed to three men. "These three were on our radar a couple years ago, but we could never catch them doing anything illegal. They just disappeared one day." Bryce turned to Heidi. "When was the last time you saw these men with your husband?"

"About six months before Lorenzo got me out of there. Before that, all the time."

"This one," Bryce pointed to the picture of a man with a long red beard and a shaved head, "is known to us as 'Big Red.' We had him under surveillance as a drug runner. But before we could catch him in the act, Big Red dropped out of sight." Bryce tapped the next picture. "This fellow changed his name more than some people change their underwear … Jacko … Milroy … Sammy … Jordash–– just to name a few of the aliases he used. He was also a master of disguise, so we discovered late into the game. We had a sting all set up one night, but the guy didn't show. No one did. Made us think we had a mole in the force somewhere.

"Anyway, this third man's name is Whitey Dommer. He was an informant, or so we thought. He fed us a bunch of info, and we were ready to close in on this big operation––a drug drop—but when we were ready to leave, Whitey never showed up. We decided to go to the location Whitey told us about, but the warehouse was deserted when we arrived. We never saw Whitey again."

Something was niggling at Bryce though, as he looked over all the information Heidi had in the box, Bryce was wondering why she hadn't come forward before. What hold did her husband have over her that had her so afraid to turn him in? But now, Cain had something she valued more than anything—her daughter. Now, Heidi was willing to take the man down.

Besides Heidi not coming forward, there was Lorenzo and his role in her escape—and the man named Pete, who executed the actual escape according to Lorenzo's plan. Why hadn't Lorenzo, who went against Cain by helping his wife escape, come forward and turn evidence against the man? The same man, it appeared, who Cain had sent someone to kill and had now disappeared after killing the man sent to kill him. The entire story wasn't making sense to the captain. He made a mental note to talk to Jack later, away from Heidi.

One of the officers knocked on the door. Jack answered it, and the officer stepped inside and announced they were finished scouring the area and had gathered and bagged several pieces of possible evidence. "We tried to dust for prints on the porch pillars, just in case the kidnapper touched them, but the rain must have washed everything clean. We'll get the bagged items back to the lab now."

"Tell them to put a rush on the results," Bryce ordered.

"Yes, sir." The young officer returned, heading back out into the dismal weather.

Bryce turned back to Heidi. "Do you mind if I take these things back to my office? I want to study your notes a bit closer."

Heidi hesitated but then relented. She was still unsure if she was doing the right thing by handing over all that damning evidence, but when Captain Wagner started talking about actually knowing some of the men in the pictures, she felt better. She needed to get her daughter back and knew she couldn't do it alone. Lorenzo was in the wind at the moment, and Pete hadn't called her back yet.

30

Cameron drove a couple miles from the house where he'd met with Cain. He was still fuming about what he was about to do. Pulling over to the side of the road, Cameron shut the car off and rested his head on the steering wheel. What he really wanted to do was cry; however, the tears wouldn't come. Only frustration and hatred—for himself and the man who was forcing him to commit acts totally against his interest. Cameron admitted he'd stepped over a line. He was desperate when he'd done so. Out of a job. Not wanting to face his wife and tell her what a failure he was. He'd failed his first marriage and didn't want to miss the mark with the second one. He didn't want to be a failure in front of his three beautiful children.

Only one thing for me to do—stop running, face the music like a grown-up, and go to the police. But what if Cain gets wind of what I'm doing before the cops find Carrie and my children? Cain is capable of evil; I see that in him. I think it was Cain who killed his brother, Abel, in the Bible—is evil in the heart of men called Cain?

Oh, my god, Colin's mother, Nancy, was supposed to pick Colin up today. She's going to be frantic when she goes to the house and Colin isn't there—no one will be there. Nancy will go to the police … oh, my God … oh, my God! Can things get any worse? I don't think I have a choice; I have to go to the police. I have to.

Cameron reached gripped the keys and turned on the ignition. The motor sputtered, then stopped. He tried again. Nothing. Smacking the steering wheel in frustration, Cameron swore. He got out of the car and went around to the front of the vehicle and lifted the hood to check out what might be wrong, not that he was any good at fixing automobiles. That was a job for his mechanic; Cameron was a pencil pusher. Well, he'd been a pencil pusher before losing his employment at the ad agency.

Searching around the engine, not knowing what he was looking for, Cameron heard a ticking sound. He leaned in closer, trying to detect the exact location of the noise. Cameron's eyes widened in terror when he noticed the small box tucked in behind the battery, a box with a timer on it. A timer that only had thirty seconds left on it as it counted down!

Cameron turned and ran as fast as he could, diving into a ditch just as the car exploded, sending debris everywhere.

Mitch had watched Cameron leave Cain's office. He was tired of doing some of the things Cain asked of him, sensing his boss was slowly coming undone at the seams. Mitch walked into the warehouse and went straight to Cain's office, entering without a knock.

Cain didn't greet his man with pleasantries, and he got straight to the point. "You did what I asked?"

"I did."

"How far down the road will he get?"

"Two or three miles."

Cain scowled. "I thought I made it clear to make sure Cameron was well away from here?"

"I wanted to ensure no one else would be hurt. Much further and Cameron would have been too close to a town," Mitch retorted. "Why'd you want to snuff the guy, anyway

… after all the trouble you went to to get his wife and kids…"

Cain snorted. "Yeah, about that. The guy was weak. He managed to get my kid for me, but when it came down to the rest of the jobs he was to do, he was soft. He failed. If he failed me once, he'd fail me again. I can't take the chance that he'll reconsider his position and go to the police." Cain looked around the office, and his gaze scanned the warehouse beyond the glass wall. "We need to move this stuff out of here now. I've located an abandoned warehouse and have called on my friends in the trucking business. They should be arriving at any time to start the move."

Mitch was shocked but tried not to display his disbelief. *I should have seen this coming. Cain is unquestionably losing it … might be time for me to cut my losses and disappear … I have enough money put away in my off-shore account that I can live quite comfortably until I find myself another gig.* Mitch grinned and asked, "What can I do to help, boss?"

"Make sure when the trucks arrive that you direct the operation. I don't want a trace of anything left behind." Cain walked over to a filing cabinet and pulled open the top drawer, taking out several file folders. "I need to shred these papers, so I'm counting on you, Mitch."

"Sure, boss … I hope you have back-ups for all those records you are about to destroy." Mitch knew Cain kept his files backed up on a thumb drive, but had no idea where that was. Something he'd need to look for when he was able to.

"That will be all, Mitch … I think I hear the trucks coming up the lane." As Cain started shredding papers, he paused a moment. "Oh, by the way, one of the trucks will pull up to the house and clean it out, as well … everything."

Cain reached into his pocket and pulled out an envelope. "Once the trucks are loaded and on their way, here is the address and further instructions. We'll meet up at the warehouse later."

Mitch took the envelope and shoved it into his pocket. He didn't like the sound of what Cain was planning and knew he was going to have to proceed with caution.

Cameron, after the initial shock of the explosion, finally stood and dusted himself off. He was thankful that his wallet was in his pocket, and the list of jobs Cain had given him to do, which would be evidence he could use to make a deal with the authorities. He climbed from the ditch and gazed at the car that was supposed to have been his coffin. There was not another vehicle in close sight, but Cameron noticed a set of headlights in the distance. The one thing he didn't want was to have any connection to the explosion. Looking toward the other side of the road, Cameron noticed a small woodlot. He climbed out of the ditch, checked to ensure it was safe to cross, then darted over to the other side.

The approaching vehicle was slowing down due to the car parts that were scattered all over the road. Cameron observed from the trees. A man exited an automobile and pulled a cell phone from his pocket. Cameron looked behind him, wanting to see how far back the woods went. He saw no end to the trees. Knowing his best bet was to get as far away as possible before the police arrived, Cameron turned and plunged into the woods, hoping it would eventually bring him out to another road. He'd call someone if he could, but the only cell phone he had was the one Cain had given him, and it had gone up in the explosion!

Mitch stood by the warehouse, directing the trucks to the back, where large overhead doors were located. Three transports came around back and one stayed up near the house. Several men piled out of the four vehicles and went to work straight away, emptying the warehouse. Once Mitch saw that everything was under control at the one location, he made his way up to the house to ensure the production was going well there, too.

Five hours later, the four transport trucks left the property. Mitch reached in his pocket and pulled out the envelope Cain had given him—his orders. Mitch's forehead creased in disgust as he read the paper. He was to wire the entire property so that if any door opened—to any building—everything would blow up. Cursing under his breath, Mitch made his way to the cabin behind the warehouse, the same one that had housed Cameron. The one where Mitch had several explosives stored. He was determined to do his work, and then, instead of waiting for Cain to call him, Mitch would buy his plane ticket and leave the country. Cain would have to handle the operation at the new warehouse himself.

31

Nancy, Cameron's ex-wife, pulled to a stop in front of Cameron's house. It was her week to have their son, Colin, and even though she knew she was an hour late to pick Colin up, Nancy couldn't help wondering why the place looked so deserted. No cars in the driveway. Curtains all drawn. No kid's toys scattered on the ground in the front yard, as was the usual case when Nancy came to get her son.

Getting out of her car, Nancy walked up the sidewalk to the front door. She pushed on the doorbell, and when there was no answer within a minute, she pushed harder. Nancy tapped her hand impatiently on the side of her leg. "Cameron … you're still irresponsible, aren't you? Made me come all this way to get our son and you didn't even have the decency to call me and tell me you weren't home." Turning on her heel, Nancy returned to her car. She was fuming by the time she reached it. "You're going to hear from my lawyer, Cameron, and I think it's time I stopped playing so nice! I'm going for full custody, and I'll think about what kind of visitation you'll be allowed."

Nancy backed out of the driveway and tore down the street, taking no heed to the park across the road and that there might be children playing in the area. She didn't notice the young mother who pulled out her cell phone. A young mother who decided she'd had enough of people speeding down the street where the park her children played in was. A young mother who dialled 911 and reported that a green Chrysler van—with the license plate number AAF7 201 was speeding in a park area where the speed zone was forty kilometres.

Less than three blocks from Cameron's house, Nancy heard the siren. When she realized the police car was after her, she pulled over and put her head on the steering wheel. The officer knocked on her window and she rolled it down. Nancy tried to explain why she was speeding: "I'm sorry, officer; I know I was speeding, but I just came from…"

"Your licence and registration, ma'am," the officer asked mechanically.

"Yes, sir." Nancy reached over and pulled a folder from the glove compartment, then took her licence from her cell phone holder and handed both pieces to the policeman.

He looked at the documents. "Do you realize you were speeding through a park area and that you might have killed a child, had one run out in front of your car? A distraught mother called you in."

"Officer," Nancy started to cry. "I think something has happened to my son … I went to pick him up from his father's house, and he wasn't there…"

"Maybe the father was out and will be back soon … that's no excuse to be speeding in a park zone. What if your kid was playing here and ran out on the street to fetch a ball or whatever…" The officer took out his ticket pad and began to write Nancy up. He handed her the ticket and, "If you have a problem with your ex, and you think he's done something with your son, then head over to the police station and make a formal complaint." The officer touched the tip of his hat, "Have a nice day, ma'am."

Nancy watched the man walk back to his cruiser. There was only one thing for her to do. Follow her gut-feeling. Something was wrong. Despite how she felt about Cameron and his unreliable habits, she had to admit that he'd never not had Colin ready when she came to pick up their son. Nancy put the car in drive and drove to the police station.

Toby couldn't believe his luck. The right turn led him to a familiar street, one that he knew for sure. He made a left turn and picked up his pace as he moved along. Another left … then a right … there was the park near Jack's house. Toby moved along faster, and soon, his home was in sight.

However, when Toby entered the house, Jack was nowhere to be seen. Toby went straight to his water dish and lapped up some water, then dove into the kibbles Jack had left for him. When he had his fill, Toby realized he was going to have to ask for help elsewhere. He set out for Heidi's.

Bear was in the backyard, and as soon as the dog saw Toby, he began to bark. Toby ignored the mutt and made his way to the front door, jumped on the window sill and meowed. He could see Heidi in the living room, sleeping on the couch. *There's no sense wasting time with her; surprised she'd be sleeping when her kid's been kidnapped! Can't figure some people out. I guess the only one left that might be able to help save Alora is the mutt!*

Toby made his way to the fence line and began meowing and circling. Bear came right up to the fence, his tail wagging furiously. *Come on, mutt … get my message … I want you to follow me. How do I get my message across to you?* Toby meowed louder and circled, moved along the sidewalk, returned to the fence, then repeating the routine.

Finally, Bear got the message. Toby watched as the dog made his way to the centre of the yard, then ran full speed toward the fence, leaping it in one bound! Bear landed a couple feet from where Toby was waiting, and as the old cat took off, the dog followed. Bear was much bigger than Toby and had to slow his pace to follow behind the cat. Toby was going slower than usual: it had been a long day, and he figured it was going to be quite a while yet before he could rest his old bones.

As Toby turned onto the street where the house with the cedar fence was, he noticed the car in the driveway—the same car that had brought Alora and him here earlier in the day. Tired as he was, Toby picked up his pace, Bear following close behind.

I hope the mutt will know what to do when we get to the house because no one will pay much attention to a cat meowing and wandering around the neighbourhood. A big fluffy white dog running about, barking up a storm—that's a different story.

Toby led Bear to the front door, hoping the dog would pick up a scent from the door where the man had pushed through with Alora. Bear sniffed all around, his tail wagging furiously as he circled.

Doesn't look like the mutt's coming up with anything. Toby was getting frustrated, but he had one more clue to give the dog before giving up. The old detective cat stood on his hind legs and scratched at the door. Bear tilted his head to the side, then suddenly realized what Toby was trying to tell him.

Bear stood on his hind legs and sniffed at the door. He started barking feverishly as he picked up Alora's scent. Bear didn't stop yapping. He even went as far as howling periodically between barks. He began racing around the house, barking as he went. The next-door neighbour came out on their porch and shouted out for the dog to be quiet. Bear ignored them; his little charge was in that house, and he was going to get to her if it was the last thing he did! His woofing increased in intensity.

Inside the house, Alora heard the barking. She sat up in bed and cried out: "Bear! My Bear is here! He's come to rescue me! Lady, open the door; let him in!" Alora jumped out of the bed where she was laying and raced into the kitchen. She started pounding on the door, not seeing the big man who was standing in the kitchen with the woman.

The man moved quickly to Alora and grabbed her away from the door. She screamed, and he put his hand over her mouth, but not before Bear heard the scream. He started barking even more furiously than before, running back around to the front door and jumping up against the wood. The man thrust Alora toward Carrie, who grabbed the child before she hit the floor, folding the hysterical youngster into her arms. Cindy, Devlin, and Colin had rushed into the kitchen when they'd heard the commotion, scared by all the screaming and barking.

Stupefied as to what to do next, the man ran a hand through his hair. Finally, realizing there was only one way to shut the dog up, the man opened the door, but not before taking a large hunting knife from a holster around his waist.

Bear was too frantic to notice what was going on beyond the door, what was in the man's hand. All he knew was that the door was opening and he had to get to Alora and save her. Bear charged. As the knife slashed through the air, the man suddenly let out a scream as a giant orange cat leaped onto his arm, knocking the blade to the floor!

Carrie moved quickly, taking advantage of the man's inattention to his captives. Seeing a frying pan on the stove, she grabbed it and swung, hitting the man square in the face. However, all he did was shake his head and then come at her, fist raised. Toby knew he had to do something more. He jumped onto the table and once again leaped at the man, this time landing on his back. Toby dug his claws in and sunk his teeth in the man's neck. Below, Bear was attacking the man's legs, ripping at the jogging pants he was wearing. Carrie swung again, this time catching the man in the chest. Between Toby, Bear, and Carrie, the man finally went down.

The neighbour, who had been shouting for Bear to stop barking, appeared in the doorway. "What the hell is going on over here?" he cried, and then, seeing the big man lying on the floor, groaning, Carrie with a frying pan in her hand standing over him, a white dog growling at the man, and a large orange cat hissing at him, the neighbour pulled out a cell phone and began to call 911. To his surprise, Carrie reached out and put her hand on his hand, stopping him from dialling.

"Please don't call the police. Everything is fine here––just a little domestic disagreement. I don't think my partner will come at me again." Carrie smiled sweetly at the neighbour.

Toby was looking at Carrie: *What the hell are you doing?! This is your chance to escape, why aren't you taking it. I'm confused. Or are you in on this whole kidnapping thing … being paid by Heidi's ex-husband … that has to be it!* Toby looked over at Bear, who was still growling at the man on the floor. *Come on, man, do the neighbourly thing! Call the police anyway … woman is lying to you … can't you tell? Do I have to do everything? Once again, Detective Toby to the rescue!*

As the neighbour turned hesitantly to leave, Toby made his move toward the doorway. Standing staunchly there, the old cat tried to bar the man from leaving. The man on the floor was still moaning, but the moans were less pronounced now. Bear was paying more attention to Alora, who had come up to him and put her arms around his neck. Two of the other three children were still standing transfixed by the scene. The third child, Toby noticed, the oldest one, had started to make his move toward the open door.

Good, an ally … at least one person in this house has some sense. Might be worth it to let the boy out and lead him to Jack. I have to save Alora before her father comes for her. Who these others are, I don't know, and at the moment, I don't care.

Colin was just about to the door when Carrie screamed at him to come back. "Colin! Where are you going?"

The boy glanced back at her: "I'm getting out of here," Colin retorted. "You can stay if you want, but I'm not scared of that man who was here the other night. I want my dad, and staying here isn't going to save him!"

Carrie was beside herself. At her feet was a dangerous man. Heading out of the door was her husband's son. Out there somewhere was her husband, probably in great danger if things fell apart here. In her kitchen were a confused neighbour, a dog that appeared to belong to the little girl—Cain's daughter—and a big orange cat that seemed to be trying to run the situation! Carrie decided to let Colin go. *Maybe he'll get the help we need … I don't know what else to do. At the least, he'll be saved … I wish…*

Colin darted out the door. Toby gazed back at the scene in the kitchen, then made his decision. He took off after the boy, running after him, meowing loudly as he tried to get the kid's attention. Colin was half-way to the stop sign when he realized the cat was following him. The boy stopped and waited for Toby to reach him, then knelt and rubbed Toby's back. Toby arched up, enjoying the finger massage. He purred, but, remembering his mission, Toby started walking away. He stopped a few feet from Colin, turned, and meowed … went a few more feet, turned, and meowed again.

"You want me to follow you, don't you?" Colin commented with a smile. "I guess I got nothing to lose. After all, I have the feeling it was you that brought that dog to the house. You know something, don't you, kitty?"

You bet my whiskers I know something … I know it all, and if you are smart, you'll just follow me. Jack will know what to do as soon as you spill the beans on what's going on; I just hope we can get back there in time to save Alora. Realizing that the kid was starting to follow him, Toby retraced his route to return home, picking up his pace as he went. *Damn … I think Jack is going to owe me the biggest fish dinner when this is all over, and I hope the cops appreciate just how smart I am. Maybe I'll even get my picture in the paper; that would be good for my detective business.* Toby's thoughts rambled as he made his way down the street.

Back at the house, the neighbour had finally left, following close on Colin's heels. He glimpsed back once, shook his head, and returned to his home. Had he stayed a minute longer in the house where Alora was, he would have seen the man on the floor sweep Carrie off her feet with his arm. The pan she held in her hand went flying and hit Bear on the head, knocking the dog back long enough for the man to regain his feet and close and lock the door.

As he turned back to Carrie, he picked up his knife and wielded it menacingly.

"Nice try, lady," the man growled. "When Cain hears about this, he's going to be furious."

Bear had recovered from the hit from the pan and made a move to attack the man. Alora cried out to him, stopping her pet in his tracks. "Please, Bear, don't!"

"Smart girl," the man grinned. "Now, lady … sit down; I'm going to tell you the way it's going to be."

Carrie's shoulders slumped in defeat. *Why didn't I let the neighbour call the police—what's the matter with me? Now, I'm right back where I started, but maybe, we aren't doomed. That cat and Cameron's son escaped, so, perhaps…* The man's next words shattered Carrie's hopes.

"I'm going to have to call the boss and let him know what's happened here," the man sneered. "Personally, I don't think it's going to go well for you, lady." The man pulled a cell phone from his pocket and pushed the button, which was the direct line to Cain.

"Cain, here."

"John, here. We have a problem."

Carrie listened as the man, whom she now knew as John, explained to Cain what had transpired at the house. Carrie knew John was getting instructions as to what to do with her and the children.

John nodded into the phone: "No problem, boss. See you soon."

Carrie's heart fell out of her chest.

John gave Carrie a big grin. "Boss wants to see you right away. Here's how it's going to work. We are all going to go out this door and get into the car. No one is going to make a fuss. ." John waved the knife. "Let's go. Children first."

Alora clung onto Bear.

"Dog stays here," Jack ordered.

Alora stamped her foot. "No! Bear comes with me. He's my friend. If you don't let him come, I'm going to scream!"

John swore, but decided it would make less of a scene if he just let the kid have the dog. "Okay, kid, you win. Let's move."

Ten minutes later, John was behind the steering wheel, his four passengers sitting quietly in the vehicle, their hands and feet bound with tape. He backed out onto the street and turned in the opposite direction of the address Cain had given him, deciding to drive to the warehouse instead.

32

Nancy made her way to the police station. Inside, she went straight to the receptionist. “I need to report a missing child,” she said, her voice shaking.

The receptionist studied the distraught woman in front of her. She reached for her phone and dialled an extension. “An officer will be with you in a moment, ma’am. Just have a seat over there.” The receptionist pointed to a row of chairs.

Nancy couldn’t sit. Instead, she paced, her eyes ever-vigilant for the officer who would be taking her statement. Finally, after what Nancy felt was forever, a female officer entered the foyer and came directly to Nancy. She put out her hand in greeting. “I’m Officer Norris … are you the lady who wants to report a missing child?”

“I am.”

“Follow me, please.” Officer Norris led the way past reception and to her desk in the central part of the station. She pulled out some forms and picked up a pen. “Your name, please,” she requested.

“Nancy White.”

Officer Norris went through the basic priority questions of name and address, etc., then asked, “What is the name of the missing child?”

“Colin … Colin MacPherson. His father and I are divorced, but we share custody—one week on, one week off. I was to pick Colin up this morning, but he wasn’t there…”

"Maybe the father just slipped out with him and wasn't back yet," Officer Norris suggested.

"No, Cameron wouldn't do that. He knows better than not to have our son ready for me because I live an hour away from Brantford. You can be sure my ex does not want to upset me!"

Officer Norris studied the woman in front of her. *Don't think I'd want to upset you either, lady. You look like a real battle-axe!* To Nancy, "Is it not possible your husband might have had an emergency? Maybe, if you return to the house now, your son will be there and all will be well. Did you think of doing that? We usually don't consider someone missing until after at least twelve hours."

Nancy stood. She was furious. She leaned over the officer's desk and snarled: "Look, Officer Norris, my son is missing. My ex-husband is missing. His entire family appears to be missing, which is not the normal behaviour of that family on exchange days. Now, are you going to take me seriously, or do I have to go over your head?"

Before Norris could answer, another officer entered the area, and the man who was following him sent a shockwave through Nancy. "Cameron!" Nancy cried out. "What the hell are you doing here? Where is my son?" She made her way to Cameron and got right up in his face. "Where is my son?" Nancy looked closer at her ex-husband and stepped back in shock. "Where the hell have you been? You're a mess."

All Cameron could do was laugh. The last person he'd expected to see at the police station was Nancy. How could his day get any worse? *Of course, Nancy would be here; she was supposed to pick Colin up today. Always the dramatic … I'll never get to see my son again when she's finished with me!*

Nancy, hearing Cameron laugh so hysterically, "What's wrong with you, Cameron? Are you on something?"

"Nancy, you have no idea," Cameron replied. "At the moment, I have more pressing matters to tend to than your temper. You'll know everything soon enough, but for now, I need to talk to this officer before something worse happens. So, if you don't mind, step aside; I'm in no mood for you today."

Shocked by her ex-husband's behaviour, Nancy's mouth dropped open. She stepped aside and let Cameron pass. He disappeared with the officer who'd been with him.

"Shut the door, please," Captain Bryce Wagner directed. As fate would have it, Cameron had arrived at the station the same time the captain was returning from Heidi's place. "Have a seat, Cameron," he added.

Cameron sat down and gazed around the office nervously. "Where do I begin … there's so much to tell."

"The beginning would be a good place." Bryce leaned back in his chair, ready to listen.

Cameron cleared his throat and took a deep breath. "A couple months ago, I lost my job, and I didn't want to tell my wife that I was such a failure. I went about my days, as usual, leaving early in the morning and returning at my standard time in the late afternoon. One afternoon, I was sitting in a restaurant/bar, and the owner came over to me and sat down at my table. The place was dead; I was the only customer. He introduced himself as Sam and asked me if everything was okay. I guess I looked as though I had a lot on my mind. Sam seemed to be a good fellow, and I thought I might be able to tell someone my troubles, even though I figured he wouldn't give a shit. He was just passing the time on a slow afternoon.

"I told Sam everything, and when I finished, the man smiled. Then he leaned forward, placed his hands on the table, and asked me what I was willing to do to get out of my mess; he might have something for me. I thought the guy was up to no good, and I should have gone with my first instinct, but I was desperate. So I listened, and when he finished talking, I thought I had found my way out of my hole. At that point, I had no idea what was actually in the packages I was to deliver. All I understood was that I was to deliver the packages and pick up the money and return it to Sam. Simple enough, right?

"Soon enough, I discovered what was in the packages, and when I saw how much money I was in charge of, I hatched a scheme … stupid of me, but at the time, I didn't think so. I put the money in an off-shore account, intending to move my family out of here as soon as possible. I'd tell them we were going for a holiday and once we got there, I'd say to them that was where we were going to live for a while. I thought I had everything under control and that I was out-smarting Sam. He'd called me a couple times, asking about the money, and I held him off by saying I was going to give it to him all in one lump sum; I still had a couple more deliveries to make. He wasn't happy but finally agreed.

"I ran off copies of passport applications for each of my family members, and the day I was taking them home to have everyone fill the papers out was the day I found a stranger in my home and my family tied up! For some reason I still can't fathom, the guy decided to save my ass. Well, to be truthful, I think he talked to someone first, and I later found out that it was the big boss who told him what to do. To make a long story shorter, this guy let my family go, but he terrified my youngest son by making him come with us while he took me to the car. It was an assurance so my wife wouldn't call the police, and he threatened if she were to call the police after her son returned, I would be a dead man.

"The guy drove me out to a place in the country. We went down a long, treed laneway, and I was taken into a big warehouse building and presented to the big boss himself. That is when I learned my fate and the fate of my family. If I didn't do what Cain—that was his name—wanted, my family was dead, and so was I. That was the last thing I wanted." Cameron looked down at the floor and the tears he'd been storing up released. His shoulders shook violently and his fists pounded on his thighs.

Bryce Wagner studied the man in front of him. *Tortured soul ... can't believe people put themselves in such circumstances, but here he is: God only knows what this man Cain has done with his family.* Bryce got up and walked over to a small refrigerator that he kept in his office. He took out a bottle of water and handed it to Cameron. "Here, have a drink and then tell me what you did. I think I already know, but I need to hear it from you." Bryce compared what he already knew about Cain from Heidi and the police records on the man.

Cameron looked at the police captain, his face strained. "I had to kidnap a little girl ... Cain's daughter ... I didn't want to ... I just didn't have a choice. Cain would have killed my family; I didn't have a choice."

Bryce put a hand on Cameron's shoulder. "Slow down, Cameron. Tell me how you did it and where the girl is."

Cameron shook his head. "That's the problem. I don't know where she is. I was to call Cain when I had the kid, and he instructed me to go to the parking lot of the Holiday Inn Express on Sinclair Blvd. When I got there, I was to give the girl to someone else; he would take her wherever Cain had instructed him. I got into another car, where I was told further instructions were in an envelope in the glove compartment."

"So, you have no idea where Cain wanted the child taken?"

"No."

"Why are you here now, besides having a guilty conscience about kidnapping a child?" Bryce was annoyed.

Cameron shuffled his position in the chair as Bryce returned to the chair behind his desk. "When I saw the list of things I had to do, it seemed simple enough. I was to collect money from people and take the cash to Cain when done. However, at the first place, I ran into a roadblock. The young man who owed Cain money lived with his aged father. The old man begged me not to hurt his son and said he would get me the money—said he'd go to the bank. When he heard how much his son owed, he blanched and asked for time; that amount was more than he could get together on such short notice. So, I told him to do what he could and that I'd be back. Then, I went to see Cain, to inform him I couldn't do what he was asking of me. It wasn't in me to hurt people physically.

"To say the least, it didn't go well. Cain was furious. He told me I had no choice but to do his bidding, and I wasn't to return until I had what he wanted. I left with a heavy heart, got in the car, and drove a couple of miles. I was desperate for a way out. I needed to think, so I pulled over to the side of the road and tried to figure a way out of my predicament. I'd shut the motor off, wanting total silence. No matter what I thought of, I realized there was no way out for me, so I turned the key in the ignition. The car wouldn't start. I tried a couple more times. Still nothing, so I got out and lifted the hood. Now, I'm not much of a mechanic—in fact, not at all. When I looked under the hood, I noticed a small box with a clock on it, and the numbers were counting down. I had thirty seconds to get away from the vehicle. I ran like hell and jumped into a ditch just as the car exploded.

"I guess I finally realized just how dispensable I was to Cain, and if he could so easily get rid of me, he'd do the same to my family. That's why I'm here. I don't have the heart to run anymore. I'm ready to face the music for what I've done. I can take you to where Cain lives."

"Did you see any sign of the child while you were at Cain's place?" the captain inquired.

"No, but there is a house on the property. She could have been in there."

Bryce picked up his phone and dialled out to dispatch. "I need a S.W.A.T team put together, pronto. I'll be in the front lobby waiting to give them instructions."

Half an hour later, Cameron was riding in the back of Captain Wagner's police car, heading to Cain's property.

33

Colin and Toby finally arrived at Toby's house. Instead of entering through his cat door, Toby jumped onto the living room window sill, hoping Jack would be watching television or reading his newspaper. Luck was with him. Toby stretched up on his hind legs and began scratching at the window and meowing. Finally, Jack looked up from his newspaper and tilted his head in surprise. A moment later, the front door opened, and Toby and Colin piled into the house.

"Who's this you have with you, Toby?" Jack asked, looking at Colin, but not expecting the old cat to answer.

Colin stood there shivering, but with a determined look on his face, he blurted out, "My name is Colin, and some bad men have my step-mom and her kids, and they brought another kid for us to look after! We got to call the police and go back and save them!"

Jack didn't need to ask anything more. He reached for his phone and dialled the police station, asking for Bryce.

"The captain's not available. He left the station a half-hour ago with a S.W.A.T. team," the dispatcher replied.

"I need to reach him now!" Jack bellowed into the phone. "This is about the kidnapping case he was investigating earlier today … I have a lead as to where the child might be."

The dispatcher cleared her throat, not sure how much she should tell Jack Nelson, even though she knew he still freelanced for the department.

"Come on … this could be a matter of life and death. A kid showed up here a few minutes ago with my cat, Toby, and he told me that he and his step-family were being held captive in a house, and someone brought them another little girl to look after. We need to get to that house before they remove the child because I have a notion that whoever is holding this family captive might be doing just that."

"Okay, Jack. I'll get a cruiser to your place immediately."

Jack hung up the phone, grabbed his jacket, and sped out the door to go and tell Heidi there was a good possibility there was a lead on where Alora might be. When Heidi opened the door, the first words out of her mouth were: "Jack, I was just coming over to tell you … Bear's missing now!" Seeing the look on Jack's face: "Tell me you've found, Alora! Please, give me some good news!" Heidi grabbed hold of Jack's hands and pulled him into the house. It was then that she noticed the young boy standing behind Jack. "Who's this?" Heidi questioned.

"This is Colin … Toby led him to my place, which leads me to believe that somehow Toby managed to discover where your Alora is, and," a hesitation, "you said Bear is missing?"

Heidi nodded.

"I'll bet my bottom dollar—like I said—Toby knew where Alora was. How he knew, we've yet to discover; but he must have returned here for help, and the only one available was your dog. Bear probably jumped the fence and followed Toby. Young Colin, here, managed to escape somehow, and Toby led him back to my place. From what he's told me so far, some guy left Alora at the house where he says he and his family were captives. I've called the police and they're sending a cruiser."

"What about your captain … is he not coming?"

"He left the station with a S.W.A.T. team; the dispatcher didn't tell me where he was going." Jack turned and looked down the street and saw the cruiser approaching. "Are you ready, Heidi?"

She nodded and grabbed a jacket.

Jack turned to Colin: "You're up, son; show us where this house is and let's go and save your family and the little girl."

Within five minutes, the cruiser stopped in front of the house with the tall cedar hedge. Everyone piled out and raced up to the front door. Jack stepped back and allowed the police officers to announce themselves, and when no one answered, they tested the door. It opened easily, revealing a colossal mess; silence greeted the group. Heidi pushed past Jack and the police and called out for her daughter.

"Alora! … Alora! … Where are you, sweetie?" Heidi screamed anxiously, racing from room to room. "There's no one here, Jack!" she hollered from down the hallway.

By now, the police and Jack had figured this out. Toby was also looking around, searching for clues. When everyone gathered back in the kitchen, Toby raced to the door and meowed. He looked back at Jack and stepped closer to the opening.

Jack looked at the officers. "Toby wants us to follow him somewhere."

Good man, Jack. You never … well, mostly never … fail to let me down. Toby took off out the door and raced over to the house of the neighbour who had tried to help. Jack motioned for everyone to follow the cat.

The door was answered by a scruffy looking fellow, holding a beer in his hand. He looked at the group of people on his porch. "What can I do for you officers?" the man slurred. "I can't remember calling the police, even though I should have. All that ruckus next door." He paused when he noticed Colin. "Glad to see the kid who got out brought some help, but…"

Jack interrupted the man in mid-sentence: "Did you see a car leave from next door?" he asked, assuming at this point that whoever had been in the house where Alora had been, had already fled.

"Yeah … a black car … give me a minute. I wrote down the licence plate number; it's on my kitchen table." The man left and returned a minute later and handed one of the police officers a piece of paper.

The officer left immediately, going to his car and radioing in to dispatch to get an APB out on the vehicle. The neighbour looked down at Toby. "That's one hell of a cat you got there, mister," he said. "The big guy in the house, the one the lady said was her partner … I didn't actually believe that … well, the big guy had a knife, and he was about to slice the white dog when it leapt through the door. That orange cat moved so fast and jumped on the guy, knocking the knife from his hand. Dog was a goner for sure if the cat hadn't moved so quickly."

Yep! That's me! A hero. But now, we need to get down to business and find this car. We need to save Alora, and if that woman is involved, we need to arrest her. If she isn't part of this whole thing, it means we have to save her! Our job's finished here. Good this guy was still sober enough to get the licence when that big man somehow got away. Toby looked up at the neighbour and meowed his approval before leaving.

Jack hung back a moment: "Thanks for your help here, and, just to let you know, we might have to get you to come down to the station to identify the people when we catch them."

"No problem, man … I guess I should have called the police right away, but the woman asked me not to. Maybe I could have saved those other kids."

Once everyone was in the cruiser, Jack suggested they drop Colin off at the police station. "He'll be safer there," Jack commented.

The driver nodded. As they pulled into the station parking lot, Nancy White was just getting into her car.

Colin pointed excitedly: "That's my mom!" he unbuckled his seatbelt and tried to open the door.

"Hang on a sec, buddy," Jack smiled. The boy had impressed Jack with his mature manner; however, every boy had a soft spot, and their mom usually triggered it. "Beep your horn," Jack directed the officer who was driving.

Five minutes later, mother and son reunited, Jack and his entourage entered the station.

34

Mitch put the final wire into place and then proceeded into the woods behind the cabin, where he had a motorcycle hidden. At the time when he'd purchased the bike and snuck it back there, he didn't know precisely why he was doing that, but now he was sure. His instincts had been right. Eventually, Cain would turn on him—like he'd been doing on almost everyone around him lately—and it appeared that now might be the time to make a quick exit. Mitch took the tarp off the bike, mounted, and fired it up. The motor purred softly.

Following a trail out of the woods, in the opposite direction of the house and warehouse, Mitch smiled. "I'll make an anonymous call to the police before I leave town," he mumbled into his helmet. "You're going down, Cain … it's time you did."

Cain was waiting for the trucks at the old warehouse he'd procured. He watched their approach and started to laugh. "I'm smarter than all of you bastards … no one is going to catch me." Cain stood in the doorway, waiting for the trucks to pull up and unload. Just as he was about to turn and go into the make-shift office he'd fashioned, Cain noticed a black car following the trucks in. He recognized the licence plate as the one on the car he'd lent to his man, John. "What the hell is he doing here?" Cain squinted and made his way to the car as it pulled to a stop beside the building.

Cain's face flushed, anger oozing out of every pore as he looked inside the vehicle. Whirling on his heel, Cain strode to the driver's door and thrust it open. He reached in and grabbed John by the scruff of the neck and pulled him out of the vehicle. "Why did you bring them here?" he demanded. "This isn't the address I gave you!"

John pulled away from Cain and cleared his throat. "Now, don't go jumping to conclusions here, boss. I had no other choice. The other place was too close to where we were, and I didn't want to take a chance on the car being recognized if the police scoped out the neighbourhood." John went on to explain to Cain what had happened back at the house, and as he talked, Cain went deeper and deeper into thought, wondering how this could occur.

"What do you want me to do with them, boss?" John asked when he finished his account of events.

Cain needed time to think. He looked into the car and swore under his breath. "Bring them into the warehouse," he ordered John as he walked away.

As the S.W.A.T. team drove down the laneway where Cameron had instructed them to turn, Captain Wagner started to get an eerie feeling in the pit of his stomach. Something wasn't right. There were deep potholes in the laneway—fresh ones. He ordered his driver to stop and then got out of the vehicle and examined the ruts more closely. Returning to the cruiser, Bryce radioed to the team behind him.

"I think we should be extremely cautious about going in here. There's a possibility the place is empty, but I believe we should send in your robot to ensure the area isn't booby-trapped."

The police cars moved forward slowly and came to a stop in the yard between the house and the large steel building. Everyone exited the vehicles, and one of the trucks unloaded a small robot. "Where should we send it first, captain?"

"Let's start with the house," Bryce replied.

The officer turned the robot on and punched a code into its hardware. Lights began to flash. Taking hold of a remote control unit, the officer swivelled the joystick around, and the robot moved toward the house. Once again, an eerie feeling shot through Bryce. When the robot was almost to the house, Bryce shouted out: "Stop!" He leaned over and picked up a rock.

Everyone was looking at the captain, puzzlement in their eyes. "What's up, Bryce?" the leader of the S.W.A.T. team asked.

Bryce held up his finger. "Everyone back!" He threw the rock through one of the house windows. "Wait now … ten, nine, eight, seven, six, five, four, three, two, one…" When Bryce said one, there was an explosion inside the house, followed intermittently by several other blasts. Then, to everyone's surprise, a line of discharges between the home and the steel building sent more shockwaves through the entire team. The squad backed up even further and took cover behind their trucks, just in time. The steel building tore apart as the explosives detonated.

Ten minutes later, there was nothing but debris where the buildings had been. Cameron was shaking like a leaf, having escaped death twice in one day. Captain Wagner was on the radio contacting the station. It was only then he learned Jack had tried to reach him with news that he had a lead on where the little girl might be.

"Where's Jack now?" the captain barked into the receiver.

"We just received a call from him … he talked to a neighbour who lives by the house the boy and Jack's cat, Toby, took the squad car to. The house is empty now, but the neighbour confirmed people were there—some children and a man and a woman. He told Jack they'd all left in a black car, but I guess the guy was concerned enough about what was going on over there that he took the licence plate down. We have an APB out on the car now."

"I need you to send the fire trucks out to…" Bryce gave the concession and closest crossing and told the dispatcher there would be a police car at the end of the laneway to guide the emergency vehicles to the property. He added that maybe an ambulance should be sent too because he wasn't sure yet if there had been any bodies in the buildings.

Half an hour later, the fire trucks rushed down the lane and came to a screeching stop in the yard. The fire chief walked up to Bryce. "Real mess here, eh?"

Bryce nodded. "All the explosives were connected so that once one went up, the rest followed like a domino effect." Bryce heard a call coming in over his car radio and excused himself from the fire chief. "Wagner, here," he yelled into the receiver.

"We got a line on the car…" the dispatcher informed, giving the captain the details. Bryce hung up and turned on his engine. "We're going for a ride, Cameron," Bryce looked to the back seat where Cameron sat for safe-keeping. "I think we might have found where your family is."

35

Jack and the officer he was with received the call just before the dispatcher informed her captain of the whereabouts of the car last seen at the house with the tall cedar hedge. Jack knew the address well, having done a stake-out in that same location when he was still on the force full-time.

"There's an old abandoned warehouse on that property," Jack informed the officer who was driving. "Hopefully, we aren't too late to save whoever needs saving."

Toby and Heidi were in the back seat, and Toby was trying to catch a couple of winks before the big take-down. *I'll be glad when this is all over … haven't had this tough of a day since getting caught in Emma's basement and seeing what she was up too. Oh, my dearest, Emma … I wonder how she's doing … I do miss her…*

"Don't put your siren on," Jack suggested to the driver. "I don't want anyone to know we're coming." Jack picked up the car radio and messaged the two cars that were following to keep their sirens off, as well.

Suddenly, Bryce's voice came over the radio. "Jack, are you there?"

"Jack, here."

"I just got notified of the location where our kidnapped child might be … are you on your way there?"

"Yep … there are also two other cruisers with me."

"Wait for me at the entrance, Jack; I'm on my way."

Cain paced in his office, looking periodically at the three children and woman that were sitting on the old couch he'd procured. Bear was tied to a post, a cord wrapped around his mouth to act as a muzzle. John hung back in the corner.

Walking up to Alora, Cain ripped the tape away from her mouth. She screamed. Growls emanated from Bear's throat and he thrust forward, stopped short of Cain by the rope around his neck.

As soon as Alora got over the shock of the tape ripping off her mouth, "I want my mommy … you are a bad man!" she screamed.

Cain laughed. "Sorry, darling … I'm your father. Don't you recognize me? I'm not a bad man."

"Yes, you are … a bad man—mommy says so."

"Well, little darling, I'm all you have right now. You're going to be staying with me from now on. Mommy stole you away from me and it took a long time for me to find you. That wasn't very nice of your mommy to take you away from your daddy." Cain reached out to touch Alora on her cheek, but she cringed away from him. "No need to be afraid of me," Cain said. "I'm not going to hurt you." Cain turned to John. "Take these other three out of here. There's a shack in the woods behind the building. Put them in there until I decide what to do with them. Take the dog, too."

"No!" Alora screamed. "I want my Bear! Don't take him away."

Cain saw an opportunity to win some points with his daughter. "You want the dog?"

Alora nodded.

"Well, tell you what … if I keep the mutt here, you'll do as I tell you." Cain paused. "Deal?"

Alora looked at her father, her eyes wide with terror. Her mommy had told her that he was an evil man, but she wasn't prepared for just how bad he was. Alora was terrified.

"Well, are you going to answer me? Are you going to be a good girl and be able to keep your dog, or should I send him out with these other three people?"

Alora wrinkled her eyebrows and started to cry, but looking at her father through her tears, she stopped, realizing he was not a man to be moved by tears. Alora swallowed hard. She had no choice but to obey. It was the only thing that was going to save her beloved pet. "I'll be good. I'll listen to you … Daddy."

Cain smiled. His daughter had called him daddy. "Good girl." Cain turned and snapped his fingers at John. "Get these others out of here."

Carrie tried to struggle as John picked her up and threw her over his shoulder; however, the tape was too tight around her wrists and ankles, and her attempts made no difference. John disappeared with her and returned a couple of minutes later for Cindy and Devlin.

"Make sure they can't get away, then get back here and help out," Cain ordered as John set off for the door a second time. "I'll decide what to do with them once we get the trucks loaded."

John nodded and left.

Cain looked at Alora. "Now, little lady, can I trust you to stay in here until I return? I have a few things to check on in my warehouse." Cain reached over, and without thinking about what Alora might do if her hands and feet were free, he cut the tape off and freed her.

Alora rubbed her wrists and then her ankles. They were raw. As soon as her father was out of the room, Alora made her move. She went straight to Bear and worked away until she got the string off his face. Bear was about to bark, but Alora put her finger to her lips. Bear knew the command. Don't bark. Then, Alora worked at the rope that was tied around Bear's neck and finally freed her dog. She returned to the couch, Bear beside her, and waited for her father's return.

36

Lorenzo had been following Cain's movements for some time. He'd watched the transport trucks loading all the goods, and had stuck around long enough to observe Mitch booby-trapping the property. While the vehicles were loaded, Lorenzo had snuck his way over to Cain's car and planted a tracker under the trunk so he'd be able to locate wherever Cain went. Then, Lorenzo called Pete, told him to grab a cab and meet him at a variety store located a few miles from Cain's place.

"What's up?" Pete asked, getting into Lorenzo's vehicle.

"Cain is on the move. Cleaning the entire warehouse out and Mitch is setting the place to blow up. I've got a tracker on Cain's car, so as soon as he moves out, we'll pick up his location and follow him."

"Don't you think it might be time to call in the cops?" Pete asked. "I mean, I know we worked for the guy and might have to serve some time … maybe not … we could make a deal … but Cain has gone over the edge."

"I've thought of calling the police, but I ain't willing to spend a day in jail for that son of a bitch. We're going to find out exactly where he's taken the goods, make an anonymous call to the cops, and then get ourselves out of the country. I've arranged everything. Got the plane tickets in my bag in the trunk. Packed a bag for you, too."

"Where we going?" Pete inquired, a slight grin on his face.

Lorenzo smiled. "Got us a little place on the beach over in Portugal. Purchased it a couple of years ago, after we got Heidi out of Cain's grasp. It's pretty run down—just a shack—but we can fix it up."

"Nice."

The tracking unit's light lit up the GPS. "Looks like our boy is on the move," Lorenzo said. "Time to go."

Half an hour later, Lorenzo knew exactly where Cain was going. He remembered locating the old warehouse for Cain when Cain thought he might need a secondary location. Lorenzo knew Cain had purchased the property but hadn't heard anything more about it.

"I know where Cain's taking the stuff," Lorenzo made conversation with Pete. "Remember that property I told you about a few years ago … the old warehouse located in a large wooded area out near the reserve?"

"Yeah … I remember you talking about that place."

"There are two ways into the property … off the main road and another one off of an old dirt lane that hadn't been in use for years. We'll park and walk in to make sure Cain is still there before we call the cops."

Pete nodded. "Sounds like a plan."

Lorenzo parked the car, so it was hidden just inside the tree line of the dirt lane. He grabbed the binoculars he'd brought, and then he and Pete followed the overgrown track to the edge of the clearing. The transport trucks were just pulling in and backing up to the warehouse. Cain's car was sitting in plain view. Pete elbowed Lorenzo in the ribs and pointed to another car that had just entered the area.

"What the hell … John?" Lorenzo squinted. "Looks like the car has some passengers … and … can't be!" Lorenzo put the binoculars up to his eyes and zeroed in on the white dog in the back seat of the vehicle.

A few minutes later, the two men hiding in the trees witnessed Cain and John having what appeared to be an argument. The back door of the car opened, and John began carrying the passengers over to the warehouse. Lorenzo's heart dropped when he saw Alora dragged from the back seat.

"Shit!" Lorenzo cursed. "Cain has Alora! We aren't going to be able to leave just yet. I wonder where Heidi is … the woman in the car wasn't her … and the other two kids … what the hell is Cain doing? Kidnapping people was never part of his deal."

Jack waited impatiently for Bryce and his team to arrive. He stepped out of the car and paced back and forth across the end of the laneway. Heidi finally joined him, unable to sit in the car any longer. Toby, who had insisted on coming along, took the opportunity of the open car door. He snuck out and made for the brush cover.

No one said I had to wait for the captain … time to take down this bastard that would dare to kidnap a little girl! Toby made his way along the tree-line that followed the laneway. Finally, he came to the clearing where the warehouse stood starkly gray in the waning light. Toby looked around, unsure how he was going to get in the building without being seen. *Lucky must be my middle name—Toby Lucky Nelson … Detective Toby Lucky Nelson! Cat superior, on the job to save the kid … and, I guess I'll have to bail out the mutt, as well!*

Noting that all the humans were busy unloading the trucks goods into the warehouse, Toby darted across the yard and slipped into the warehouse. He found an excellent place to hide behind some piled boxes, where he could scope out the area and see if he could locate Alora. Toby's eyes lit upon a man standing in the centre of the building and instantly knew who it was. As he continued scanning, Toby noticed a room across the way. He had a cat feeling that might be where they were holding Alora. To his dismay, though, there was no way to reach the room without the possibility of being seen.

Well, guess I'll just have to take my chances. I've had a rest, so I should be good to go. If I'm going to prove to be the best detective the Brantford Force ever had, I have to believe in myself. Okay, here goes ... I got this!

Toby padded out from behind the boxes and dashed across the room. He'd almost reached his destination when he heard a voice boom out.

"What the hell is that cat doing here?" John yelled as he returned to the warehouse.

Cain turned, startled by his employee's comment. "What cat? What are you talking about, John? Are you afraid of an old stray cat? There's probably several of them in the woods around here."

John pointed to where Toby was, sitting in front of the closed door of the office. "That ain't no stray, boss. That's the cat that attacked me back at the house. Leapt right on my arm and knocked the knife from my hand."

Cain snorted sarcastically. "What an imagination you have, John. How the hell would that particular cat get here from Brantford? Get a grip, man, and get to work. We need to get this stuff unloaded and move out of here."

John shook his head. "No, boss. I won't ever forget that cat. And if he's here, I'll bet my bottom dollar he's not alone!"

Cain threw a disgusted look at John, laughed, and turned away.

Toby took the opportunity to try and find a way out of his predicament. He slipped around the corner of the office, and once again, luck was with him. A hole at the bottom of the back wall, just big enough for him to wiggle through, presented itself. Toby didn't care how it got there; it was just good luck that it was! Inside the room, Toby saw Alora and Bear sitting on a worn-out couch. They hadn't seen him yet, but Toby knew Bear sensed there was someone in the room. He began to whine, but Alora put her finger to her lips and told him to hush. Toby took the opportunity to hide under the old oak desk.

Bryce finally arrived with his backup team. They pulled to a stop just before the laneway, lining up along the side of the road. Bryce exited his vehicle and made his way over to Jack. "I think it best we walk in."

Jack turned to Heidi. "I think it would be better if you stayed here," he suggested.

Heidi shook her head. "No way, Jack. My daughter is in there, and I want to see the look on Cain's face when he gets arrested. I want him to know it was me who helped take him down! Don't even try to stop me!"

Jack opened his mouth to protest.

"Don't, Jack. I'm coming, and that's final!" Heidi swivelled around and started down the lane.

Bryce chuckled. "Feisty lady, eh, Jack? I guess we better follow her before she gets there and makes the arrests without us. Don't ever mess with a mother whose child is in danger—that's what I was always told." Bryce motioned to the waiting team, and together the police followed Heidi down the lane.

Cameron had watched the entire scene from the back of the cruiser. Everyone seemed to have forgotten about the man who'd led them to Cain's property. With all the police gone, Cameron wondered if he should just make a run for it now. After all, he had committed a serious crime and he figured his family would be better off without him.

Toby heard the office door open, and he peeked out from the narrow opening at the bottom of the desk. Two men. One of them he recognized—John. *The other one must be Cain—nasty looking fellow. Looks mad … crazy eyes.*

"Cain, I tell you, that cat must be in here … nowhere else to go."

"John, I'm not going to let a stray cat's presence in this warehouse send me into a panic … get a grip, man!" Cain walked over to Alora and Bear. He didn't even think about the fact that Bear was no longer tied and muzzled. "Alora, dear, did you see a big orange cat come in here?"

Alora shook her head. Bear laid his head on Alora's leg. He growled softly as Alora stroked her pet, trying to calm him.

"See, John, no kitty here. Now, let's get back to work." As the two men left the office, Cain asked John if the woman and her two kids were secure. Toby saw John nod and heard him tell Cain that the bitch and her brats wouldn't be going anywhere.

Oh no! Maybe I was wrong about the woman in the house. Perhaps she was afraid of something, and that's why she didn't want the cops called.

37

Lorenzo put the binoculars down and scratched his head. There was no way he and Pete could take on Cain and all his men and hope to rescue Alora, let alone get themselves out alive. "If I remember correctly," Lorenzo's mind began to clear, "there's a shack behind the warehouse. I bet that's where Cain will store his prisoners until he gets his product unloaded." Lorenzo motioned for Pete to follow him.

"Bingo!" Lorenzo whispered as he and Pete came upon the shack. The sound of groaning was filtering through the thin walls.

Lorenzo was ready to rush into the building, but Pete grabbed his arm. "Not a good idea, my friend. We don't know who all is in there, or what they might be packing."

Patting his pocket, Lorenzo grinned and pulled out a shiny black gun. "Have you met Lucifer? Won't be the first time he's sent someone to hell!"

Pete couldn't help chuckling. "Okay, my friend, I'm right behind you." Pete reached down and took a gun from an ankle holster, readied it for action, and followed Lorenzo cautiously up to the cabin.

Lorenzo peered through some cracks in the wooden walls, squinting to get a good look at who was inside. He directed Pete to slide down to the ground with him, and the two men sat quietly for a moment, contemplating.

"Did you see Alora?" Pete questioned, a hint of nervousness in his tone. He tried to settle the butterflies in his gut, which indicated there might be someone else in the room besides Cain's captives.

"Can't see Alora," Lorenzo whispered. "But the woman and two kids are there, and they've got packing tape on their wrists, ankles, and mouths." Lorenzo stood again and made his way to the door, opening it slowly, his gun ready in case he'd missed another entity in the room.

As the door squeaked open, Lorenzo noticed the woman looking his way, her eyes wide with fright. She struggled against her restraints. Lorenzo put a finger to his lips, cautioning the woman to be quiet—in case there was someone else in the room. He motioned Pete inside and then ensured the woman and kids were the only cabin inhabitants, went directly to the woman. Taking a knife from his pocket, Lorenzo cut the tape from her ankles and wrists.

"This might hurt," Lorenzo informed as he grabbed hold of the edge of the tape on the woman's mouth. She winced in pain but didn't cry out.

While Lorenzo was freeing Carrie, Pete was seeing to the children. Once they were free, they ran to their mother and fell into her arms.

Lorenzo looked at the touching scene. "Who are you?" he inquired.

Carrie paused, unsure if this man was safe to talk to, or if Cain had sent him to finish her and the children off, and the guy was just being nice about it. Trying to throw her off-guard. *What do I have to lose … the children and I are either dead or, someone sent us a saviour.*

"My name is Carrie MacPherson. My husband tried to cross Cain, your boss…"

"Cain isn't my boss!" Lorenzo said testily. "At least not for a long time. So you and your kids were taken as insurance for your husband to do Cain's bidding …do I have that right?"

Carrie nodded.

"There was a little girl and a dog in the car with you; do you know where they are?" Lorenzo squatted beside Carrie.

"The last I saw them, Cain had them in a room in the big warehouse," Carrie replied.

Pete spoke up now. "Cain's not going to hurt his kid, Lorenzo. Let's get these three somewhere safe and then go back for Alora and Bear."

Lorenzo ran his hand along the back of his neck. " Good idea, Pete." He turned to Carrie. "Can you walk?"

She nodded again.

"Good." To Pete, "You grab one of the kids; I'll carry the other one. It'll be faster that way. We can put them in our car until we get Alora. They'll be safe there."

Pete nodded, picked Devlin up, and stepped out the door. However, years of being diligent caused him to pause. He turned back to Lorenzo. "Someone's coming."

The words were no sooner out of his mouth when John walked out from the tree line. As soon as he saw Pete and Devlin, John drew his gun. "What the hell!" John shouted across the clearing. "Where do you think you're going with the kid?" Then, he glimpsed Lorenzo and Cindy, and Carrie standing back in the shadows of the shack. "What the hell!" John repeated and rushed forward, brandishing his gun threateningly.

Pete slowly set Devlin down and lifted his arms in assumed surrender. He smiled. Lorenzo knew how Pete operated. Cool. Calm. Collected. Lorenzo knew John was a dead man.

John, thinking he had the advantage, grinned. "Hand them over to me, and I'll let you go."

Pete's smile widened. "You think so?" Before John could make another move, Pete's gun was smoking, the sound of the shot echoing through the woods.

Cindy screamed. Devlin ran to his mother. Pete turned casually: "We need to make haste. No idea who might have heard the gunshot."

Lorenzo calmed everyone down, then herded them in the direction of where he'd left his car.

38

Cain thought John was taking far too long to get back to the warehouse. "It shouldn't take this much time to snuff out that woman and her brats," Cain mumbled. He'd decided to tie up all his loose ends. With Cameron dead—blown up in the car—there was no need to keep his family alive.

When the gun went off, there'd been so much noise in the warehouse that the shot wouldn't be heard inside the building.

Cain entered the office and pulled a chair up in front of the couch where Alora and Bear were sitting. Toby watched from under the desk, not knowing what he could do to help his friends.

"Well, Alora, it won't be long before I finish out there. Then we can go. How'd you like to take a holiday with me? Maybe to a beautiful tropical island where you can swim in the ocean, and Bear can run free on the shore?"

Cain held his temper at bay as he observed the scowling eyes behind the fake smile his daughter was sending him. *I'll drown the mutt when you aren't looking—it'll be easy. Then I'll mould you into a good little girl.*

Finally, getting no genuine reaction from Alora, Cain stood and left the room, slamming the door on his way out. *Little bitch … can't wait to teach her a lesson, and unlike her mommy dearest, Alora will be eating out of my hand before her next birthday!*

Toby, ever the vigilant detective, observed Cain's body language and knew in his heart that the man, despite his sweet tone toward Alora, didn't mean anything he said. Toby noticed the look of hatred in Cain's eyes as he left the room, and also that the lock hadn't clicked into place. Waiting a few more moments before crawling from his hiding place, Toby made his presence known.

"Toby!" Alora exclaimed. "How did you get here?"

Bear's tail thumped on the couch cushion, but he remained fast beside his young mistress.

Toby made his way across the room and jumped up on the couch. He rubbed his head in greeting against Alora's shoulder, as there wasn't any room on her lap. Once the nicety of saying hello was over, Toby climbed on the back of the couch and peered out the dust-laden window.

Looks like the unloading is almost done, which means Cain will be taking Alora out of here. Where the heck are you, Jack? Toby circled a couple of times, then jumped back down beside Alora. *I need to get the kid and dog out of here … but to where … and how to leave the building without being seen?*

Toby pushed harder on Alora's shoulder this time, jumped off the couch, and meowed. He looked back at Alora, meowed again, then headed for the door and scratched at it.

Alora was quick to take the hint. "Come on, Bear," she ordered. Together, they made their way over to Toby. Alora turned the doorknob and slowly opened the door.

Toby pushed forward, wanting to be the first one to exit so he could check the lay of the warehouse. Everyone was still busy, and Cain was standing amid the turmoil. Toby heard a truck engine start, and one of the transports pulled away, leaving only two left to finish unloading, and they were almost empty, too.

Toby searched the area. His eyes lit on a door at the end of the narrow hallway. Toby turned, meowed, and then started toward what he hoped would be freedom. *Guess I have to save the day myself … Jack's taking forever to get here!* Toby glanced back to make sure Alora and Bear were following. *Good girl. Now, all I can hope for is the door is unlocked, and that it leads to outside—and freedom!*

Luck was with the trio. The door was cracked open, and Toby pushed through into the fresh air. Alora and Bear were close on the old cat detective's paws. Once outside, Toby paused and looked around. Noticing what appeared to be a trail into a wooded area, Toby took off in that direction, knowing his companions would follow.

39

Jack caught up to Heidi and took hold of her arm. "It's one thing to come with us, Heidi, but you need to let the police lead the way."

Heidi was about to protest but thought better of it. In her heart, she knew Jack was right. "Okay, but I'll be there when you take Cain down … don't deny me that!" Heidi fell in behind Jack as the police moved forward toward their destination.

Lorenzo and Pete secured Carrie and her children in their vehicle, ordering them to stay put. "I have to go back for Alora," Lorenzo informed them. "We'll be back as soon as possible."

Carrie watched her two saviours head back to the warehouse. She reached out to her children, wrapping her arms around the most precious people in her life.

Cain hadn't gotten as far as he was by being careless. He'd begun to get a gut feeling that something was amiss, so he called upon a couple of his men to stand post at the edge of the clearing. "Hide in the trees and keep watch," Cain ordered. "I don't want any surprise visitors."

It was niggling at Cain that John hadn't returned yet, so Cain motioned to the driver of the empty truck. "Max, I need you to go and see what's taking John so long; he should have looked after that woman and her brats by now."

Max nodded and set out for the back door of the building—the same one Toby, Alora, and Bear had exited not long before.

As Toby came to the end of the trail, he stepped into the clearing and noticed the cabin, its door wide open. What he didn't detect immediately was John's lifeless body. Too late. Alora saw it and screamed!

Max heard the scream as he entered the woods. He picked up his pace, racing toward the sound. Toby and Bear both heard the sound of feet, and Bear pushed Alora toward the cabin. She stumbled forward and was safely inside just as Max burst into the clearing. He saw John's body immediately. And there, beside the corpse, sat a big orange tabby cat cleaning behind his ears.

Toby watched warily the man who'd come through the trees. He noticed the guy was packing a gun, and Toby groaned as Max pulled the weapon from his waistband and swung it around the clearing. Toby glanced toward the cabin to make sure Alora was safe, then stood and hissed at Max.

Max scowled. "I ain't interested in you, kitty," he mumbled as he began heading toward the open cabin door.

Toby made his move, attacking from behind, taking Max by surprise. "What the hell!" he shouted angrily as Toby's claws and teeth sunk into his leg.

Need you, Bear … can't take this big fellow down by myself!

As though Bear heard Toby's thoughts, he appeared in the doorway of the cabin, his lips curled in a growling snarl.

Max was confused. He tried to point his gun at the dog but was kept off-balance by the orange cat attacking his legs.

Bear moved forward, still growling, his muscles in attack mode. Max tried to shake Toby off his leg, then realized the cat had already released his hold. However, what Max didn't discern was the tag-team. He glanced over his shoulder, and when he looked back at the dog, Bear was even closer.

Suddenly, it dawned on Max what—who—the animals were protecting. Cain's daughter. As this thought raced through his mind, Max glimpsed Alora, peering out a cracked window. *Boss will appreciate me bringing him back his kid.* Max, finally getting a grip on his balance, and realizing the cat had backed off, pointed the gun directly at Bear. *Take the mutt out with a bullet and the cat with a good swift kick to the gut.*

However, Max was too late! As his finger squeezed the trigger, the animals attacked simultaneously. Bear leaped through the air, zeroing in on Max's throat. Toby struck the intruder from behind. The gun blasted off into thin air and then went flying to the ground. Max fell backward, Toby getting out of the way just in time before the bulky body hit the ground. Bear's teeth closed over the man's throat, but there was no more need to take his attack any further. A pool of red was spreading along the ground around Max's head, where it had connected with a jagged rock jutting out of the earth.

Alora ran out of the house and threw her arms around Bear's neck. Toby pushed his way in, too, in need of a little praise for his part in the take-down. Despite the joy of overcoming the intruder, the trio didn't hear the other sets of footsteps approaching, and by the time Bear and Toby realized they were being invaded again, it was too late. Alora was grabbed up by Cain, and the two men who were with their boss struck Alora's protectors down with a massive boot to their stomachs.

Toby found himself flying through the air, landing on his side in a pile of pine needles. Bear yelped in pain, trying to regain his feet before Cain disappeared with Alora. But he was too late and met with another boot in his gut in the attempt. Toby, on the other hand, was able to recover and slip out of the clearing, and, despite his body still shaking from the trauma he'd just experienced, he was able to shadow Cain.

Cain's intuition had told him to park his SUV behind the building. He'd ensured when he purchased the property that there was more than one exit. One he would use now––and quickly. As he opened the back door of the vehicle, Cain heard a loud noise coming from the other side of the building. The voices of police ordering his men to the ground permeated through the air. Cain motioned to the two men who were with him. "Get in … we need to get out of here—pronto!"

As Cain's back was turned, he didn't notice Toby slip into the SUV and crawl under the back seat. Alora smiled despite her fear. Once again, Toby was going to ensure her rescue.

40

Lorenzo and Pete had almost run into the police when they returned to the warehouse. They hung back as the force burst into the building, yelling for everyone to get down on the ground and put their hands behind their heads.

Heidi stuck close to Jack, her eyes searching for Alora. And for Cain. She couldn't see either one of them anywhere. "He's gone, Jack," she hollered above the din. "He's taken Alora and gone. We'll never find her now. Cain has too many out-of-country connections…"

Jack grabbed hold of Heidi's shoulders and looked into her eyes. "We'll find her, Heidi; Cain can't have gone far. Have faith. In fact," Jack paused, "I have a feeling someone exceptional is with Alora right now, ensuring no harm comes to her."

Heidi tilted her head to the side, looking at Jack with questioning eyes.

"Toby," Jack informed. "He disappeared from the car as soon as we arrived, and knowing Toby the way I do, he's on the job. He's either found Alora and is with her, or, at the least, close by her.

Jack noticed Bryce approaching. "Any sign of Alora?" he questioned. "Or Cain?"

"Not that we've been able to see," Jack replied. He surveyed the interior and noticed the office at the back corner. "I'm going to check that room," he informed, pointing across the warehouse.

Heidi followed Jack into the room, and her face showed disappointment at not finding Alora. "She's not here," Heidi choked, tears crowding her eyes.

"But I think she has been," Jack commented as he bent over and picked up a chunk of white hair. "Bear's fur." Jack walked around the room, making his way to the desk. He peered under the desk and saw some orange hairs caught in a sliver of wood. "Toby was here too," Jack added, standing and returning to Heidi.

Taking the distraught mother by the elbow, Jack ushered her from the room. He peered down the narrow hallway and saw the door, which was ajar. Experience had taught Jack never to go it alone when there was even the slightest possibility of trouble. "I want you to stay with Bryce," Jack said to Heidi. "I'm going to take Officer Greg with me and check out behind this place."

Heidi didn't like that idea, but Jack gave her no choice. She watched impatiently as Jack and Officer Greg went out the back door. The first thing Jack saw coming out of the woods was Bear. The dog was limping.

But, there was no Alora. No Toby.

41

Lorenzo and Pete watched the chaos taking place in the warehouse. "I don't think the girl is in there," Pete commented.

"I believe you're right." Lorenzo pointed to his right. "If I know Cain, he has an alternative plan in case things go south, and if my memory serves me correctly, there's another way out of this property. Follow me."

As Lorenzo and Pete rounded the back corner of the warehouse, they came face to face with Jack, Greg, and Bear.

Intuition told Jack that the two men who had appeared were not part of Cain's current crew. He remembered the description Heidi had given him of her friend, Lorenzo. "Are you Lorenzo?" Jack asked quickly, pointing to the man in question.

Lorenzo nodded. "And you are?"

"Jack. Heidi's neighbour."

Getting directly to the point, "I take it that you didn't find Alora in there?" Lorenzo motioned toward the warehouse.

Jack shook his head.

Lorenzo pointed to some fresh tire tracks. "Follow me. I know where Cain's going. What he doesn't know, though, is that during a storm, about three years ago, part of this road was washed away. He's not going to get far in his vehicle."

Heidi appeared in the back door opening. When she saw Lorenzo, her face lit up, and she ran to him, throwing her arms around his waist. Lorenzo blushed at the display of affection. “Have you found Alora?” Heidi asked, anticipation mounting in her voice.

“No,” Lorenzo shook his head, “but I think I know where Cain has taken her.” He turned to Jack. “Let’s not waste any more time.” With those words, Lorenzo led the way to the narrow lane.

Cain cursed and hit the steering wheel as he brought the SUV to a stop. About twenty feet of the lane was washed away. Trees crowded the sides, and a thick cover of vegetation had sprung up in the earth. Cain got out of the vehicle and motioned to his men to get some bags from the back, and then follow him. Reaching into the back seat, Cain pulled Alora out and flung her over his shoulder.

Alora struggled against her father. “Let me down!” she cried and started pummelling his back. “I want my mommy!”

Toby watched the scene from his hiding spot under the seat. *Hope the guy leaves the door open or I’m trapped in here … need to follow them … or maybe go back and get Jack and a couple of those cops he hangs with … like I’ve said before, there’s only so much a cat can do alone! Even one as superior as me!*

For Toby’s luck, Cain wasn’t interested in wasting time by shutting the SUV door. He had his hands full trying to control Alora, who continued to struggle. Toby waited until Cain and his men were out of sight before he exited the vehicle. He stood on the path for a moment, pondering his next move.

Should I follow Cain, or go back for Jack? Damn! I know I can't save Alora by myself, so this shouldn't even be a question. Toby took off toward the warehouse. *You better be on your way, buddy; we can't lose Alora now. If Cain makes it out to the highway and calls one of his buddies, he just might escape, and we'll never see Alora again!*

Toby quickened his pace.

42

Bear picked up on the tension of the humans around him, and despite his sore ribs, Bear set a quick pace, racing ahead of Lorenzo. The group hadn't gone far when Bear spotted an orange furball speeding toward them. Bear barked. Toby stopped, took a breath, then meowed.

Good, the mutt is still alive. For a dog, Bear showed great courage trying to save Alora. He was a big help when he jumped on the big guy, knocking him over—good thing for the rock—I couldn't have pushed the man over!

Bear reached Toby and began covering him with wet doggy kisses. Toby cringed at the slobber that was caking his fur. He struggled away from Bear and hissed at him. *No time for this, mutt … we have to save Alora!*

Jack, noticing Toby's discomfort, moved forward quickly, and took hold of Bear's collar. "Back off, boy; we need to let Toby lead us to Alora."

Thank God, Jack! At least you know what's going on here! Toby, knowing now that the group of humans would follow him, turned back the way he'd just come. Despite how tired he was, somehow, the old detective cat found an extra spurt of adrenaline as he raced to save the little girl from her father.

Cain struggled along the edge of the washed-out trail. His two men followed him, their weapons drawn in case of unwanted visitors. When Cain reached the actual roadway again, it wasn't in much better shape; the weather had wreaked havoc on it, as well. A couple times, Cain stumbled on an extruding rock, almost dropping Alora. She'd finally stopped struggling, but he could hear her crying softly. Cain didn't care. He'd toughen the kid up soon enough once he got her away from her mother.

"If my memory serves correctly, boys," Cain hollered back to his men, "there's an abandoned house not too far up here. When I bought this property, I evicted the tenants that were living in the house. We can stop and hide inside while I call for a car to pick us up."

Within moments, as Cain had predicted, the house appeared. Most of the windows were broken, and the majority of the paint had flaked off. The steps leading to the front door were half missing, and what ones were left, looked to be splintering. Cain's foot almost went through one of the wooden slats as he made his way onto the veranda.

Once inside, Cain deposited Alora on a dust-heavy couch that the previous tenants had left behind. "Stay put," he ordered the frightened child. He turned to his men: "I want one of you to keep an eye on the front of this place; the other on the back … can't take any chances right now."

Alora was watching her father as he took his cell phone from his pocket and began dialling. She noticed how his hands were shaking, and even at her young age, Alora sensed he was nervous. She closed her eyes and whispered a prayer to Jesus for Toby to have made it safely away, and that he was bringing help.

43

Toby stopped at the edge of the washed-out trail. Bear crowded in beside him and began sniffing the ground. Suddenly, he started circling and barking. His tail was wagging furiously.

"Bear has picked up Alora's scent," Heidi informed the group.

"I believe you're right," Jack returned. "Okay, Bear," Jack hollered to the excited dog. "Show us the way."

Taking the order in stride, Bear took off across the washed-out road, followed by Heidi, Jack, and Greg. Despite wanting to be the leader, Toby was tired, still recovering from so much running. He trailed behind, keeping the group in view as best as possible.

Might be a good idea to stay apart from them—in case things go south when we find Cain.

Cain's men knew how to seclude themselves while keeping a lookout for their boss. Kurt and Luigi had been part of Cain's crew for ten years, and they liked their job, mainly because it paid very well—enough to overlook the fact they were on the wrong side of the law.

Kurt, who was hiding in the trees at the front of the house, was the first to hear the pounding footsteps approaching. He pulled his cell phone from his pocket and sent a quick text message to Cain, and another one to Luigi.

Cain cursed when he saw the message. He needed more time. His friend was on the way, but wouldn't be able to reach the location for at least another twenty minutes. Cain glanced over at Alora, still curled up on the couch. The child was his way out of here; no one would dare take him down if the kid was in his arms. A flapping sound from the back of the room made Cain look to where the noise came from—an open window—an escape route. His way out. Kurt and Luigi would hold the fort while he got away. If they went down, Cain wasn't afraid of anything. He had a lot of dirt on them that could increase any prison time they might have to serve for just being part of his gang. Having crucial, incriminating information on his men had been Cain's way of staying out of prison.

Quickly, Cain made his decision. He strode to the couch and grabbed Alora by the arm, jerking her to her feet. "Time to go, sweetheart."

Alora cried out in pain as her father's fingers dug into her flesh.

Cain dragged her to the open window. He noticed Luigi lingering nearby and motioned to his man as he passed Alora out the window. "Watch the kid while I get out," Cain commanded.

Luigi grinned and took Alora from Cain. Alora struggled against the big man and pummelled at his chest. Luigi laughed: "You ain't going anywhere, little girl, but with your daddy."

Once Cain was through the window, he brushed the dust from his pants, then reached for Alora. "Buy me some time; Franko will be picking me up shortly. You and Kurt know what to do if you get out of here."

Luigi nodded. But he wasn't smiling anymore. He knew things were falling apart, and he also knew there was no escaping this time. If the police were hot on Cain's trail, anyone connected to the man would be going down with their boss. It might be time to consider a deal was the thought that raced through Luigi's mind. He watched as Cain headed into the woods in front of the house, heading toward the road.

Kurt wasn't ready to be caught by the police. After sending the text messages, he'd made his way to the back of the house where Luigi was. Kurt witnessed Cain taking off with Alora and knew instantly that he and Luigi were on their own. "Maybe it's time to cut our losses and disappear," he mumbled as he made his way over to his partner. "Let's get out of here," he commented.

"Cain wants us to keep the cops busy until he gets away with the girl," Luigi informed.

"I don't give a shit what Cain wants at this point!" Kurt retorted. "I ain't going to jail for him. You know as well as I do, Cain has been losing it lately. We both knew it was only a matter of time before he got caught."

"I know, but," Luigi wasn't entirely convinced yet, despite the misgivings going through his mind.

The sound of barking made Luigi's decision for him. He followed Kurt, who had already taken off through the woods, zigzagging away from the trail they'd come in on, and not taking the same direction as Cain.

Bear burst into the clearing in front of the house, barking furiously as he advanced toward the open front door. Jack, Greg, Lorenzo, and Pete were close on his heels. Heidi wasn't far behind. Greg pulled his gun from its holster and waved it around the empty room. Bear ran to the couch and barked frantically, jumping up on the blankets and turning around and around.

"Cain was in here with Alora," Heidi said, moving forward to where Bear was. "Find Alora, Bear," she instructed the dog.

Bear jumped off the bed and put his nose to the floor, heading to the open window. His bark increased in intensity as he put his paws on the windowsill and picked up Alora's scent.

"Looks like Cain went out the window," Jack commented and turned back to the door. "Let's go; this way."

By the time the humans arrived behind the house, Bear was out the window and picking up the scent of the man who had kidnapped his little friend.

Kurt and Luigi paused at the sound of Bear's barking. They looked around, trying to detect a quicker way out of the woods. "Maybe we should head back to the warehouse," Luigi said, not thinking about what he was saying.

Kurt scowled. "No way, man. If the cops are here, you can bet they are all over the warehouse. We need to look after ourselves now and not worry about anyone else." He paused a moment, looking back at Luigi. "You coming with me or going to jail?"

Luigi hesitated, but for only a moment. He'd served time before and was in no hurry to return to living behind bars. "I'm with you, buddy. Let's get out of here."

44

Toby was still making his way through the woods when he saw Kurt and Luigi. Slinking behind a thick bush, Toby watched the two men, not daring to make a sound. *If these two are here, that means Cain and Alora can't be far ... but why aren't they all together? Cain must have left them behind to delay us while he got away. Looks to me like Cain's men might be deserting him.*

As Kurt and Luigi disappeared into the woods, Toby made his way from the hiding spot. He decided to follow Jack but keep to the woods, skirting the house he'd noticed through the trees.

Jack and his companions soon enough caught sight of Cain and Alora. Cain was sitting on a massive boulder at the side of the road, and he was on his cell phone talking with someone, not appearing too happy with his conversation. Before Jack could stop Bear, the dog charged.

Cain looked up in shock, dropped his phone, and quickly pulled a revolver from his coat pocket. He wrapped his other arm around Alora's neck, pointed the gun at Bear, and pulled the trigger, catching Bear in the shoulder as the animal leapt toward him.

"Bear!" Alora screamed and struggled in her father's arms, kicking at him with every ounce of strength she could muster.

"Settle down, sweetheart, or I'll put another bullet in that dog of yours," Cain hissed in Alora's ear.

Seeing that Bear was still moving, struggling to get to his feet, despite the blood pouring from his wound, Alora realized her father wouldn't hesitate to finish the job. She also sensed that Bear was not alone and was rewarded with the sight of three people crashing through the woods. Greg pointed his gun straight at Cain. Jack had to hold Heidi back as she tried to run to her daughter.

"Not a step further," Cain shouted. "I'll be leaving here with my daughter and you won't be stopping me."

Heidi found her voice: "Let Alora go, Cain. You don't care about her now—you never did."

The echo of Cain's laugh filled the area. Jack was shocked at how evil the man sounded. He noted the madness in Cain's eyes, and Jack knew from experience that a madman was a dangerous creature!

Lorenzo stepped forward. "Why are you doing this, Cain? Heidi's right. You never cared for the kid. You're only using her as a pawn to make your escape."

Cain cleared his throat and sneered at Lorenzo. "Well, well, look who has crawled out of hiding. You should be dead, shouldn't you?" A brief pause. "And may I remind you—my wife's name is Jennifer, not Heidi."

"Not anymore, Cain," Lorenzo retorted sarcastically. "And as you can see, I'm not dead. Your man missed me and shot a round of bullets into some pillows—before he took one to the head. You might be joining him if you don't let the girl go," he added.

"Tell you what, Lorenzo, you and all your buddies back out of here, and I'll make sure Alora lives long enough to grow up."

Lorenzo was a big man and he knew if he caused enough of a confrontation, it would distract Cain from noticing what Pete was doing. At least, Lorenzo hoped Pete would get the message and make a move. Lorenzo stepped ahead of the group with the pretence that he was going to check on Bear. "Let me look at the dog, Cain … at least stop the bleeding."

"Let the mutt die," Cain spit angrily.

"You don't want to do that," Lorenzo moved even closer to Bear. "You know how much Alora loves her dog. Do you expect her to ever care about you if you kill her pet?"

Cain wasn't buying it. "Get back, Lorenzo. I can just as quickly put a bullet in you as I did the dog! Personally, I don't give a shit if the kid ever cares about me." Cain waved the gun: "Now, get back with the others."

Lorenzo backed up to re-join the group, now minus one. He breathed a sigh of relief.

Toby heard the gunshot. *Oh, no! Jack! Have you gone and got yourself shot again! I'm coming, buddy … I'll save you…* Toby pushed forward, putting all the determination into his pace that he could. *Going to need an entire year to recoup from this case!*

As Toby closed in on the standoff scene, he paused and studied the situation. Cain was holding onto Alora and pointing a gun at Toby's friends … Officer Greg was slowly setting his weapon on the ground … Jack was still standing, holding Heidi by the arm … Heidi was struggling to get free, and Toby could see the anger on her face—and fear—as she looked at Cain … Bear was laying on the ground, blood soaking into the soil by his shoulder.

Toby looked around; his eyes lit upon a large oak tree just behind where Cain was standing. Toby moved quickly toward the tree, making sure he stayed hidden from anyone's view. He circled to the back of the tree and began his climb, noting a large lower branch where he could get a decent view of the situation.

Good thing I'm a cat ... we have stealth down to an art! Situation doesn't look too good for Alora. Hmmm... Toby squinted and inched further down the branch.

Cain was backing away slowly from where Jack, Greg, and Heidi were standing. The trio didn't dare to move against Cain, who was now holding the gun to Alora's waist. The sound of a car horn echoed through the stillness. "My ride is here," Cain informed. "I'd suggest you guys remain where you are if you don't want to be responsible for Alora's demise."

Toby saw his window of opportunity to do something was closing fast. If he didn't make his move now, Alora would be gone, and Heidi might never see her daughter again.

45

Pete, who was known for his cat-like movements, scurried away quickly and quietly. He veered in the direction of the giant oak tree where Toby was hiding and pulled out his gun. Toby looked down at the base of the tree at the sound of Pete's approach. The old cat returned his attention to Cain, recognizing Pete as a friend. Toby let out a soft meow, letting Pete know he had backup. Well, in Toby's mind, Pete was his backup!

Toby crept further down the branch and set his body in pounce mode. He looked back at Pete momentarily. Pete nodded as though he knew precisely what the cat was going to do. Toby leaped, sailing through the air, landing directly on Cain's arm—the arm holding the gun to Alora.

Cain hollered in shock and released his hold on Alora. Jack raced to the child and grabbed her up in his arms. Pete and Lorenzo were on Cain in seconds—Lorenzo knocking his old boss to the ground, ordering him not to move. Pete shoved a pistol to Cain's temple. Heidi raced to Jack and folded Alora into her arms, both of them crying tears of relief.

The sound of tires squealing away came from the road. "Sounds like your ride is leaving, Cain," Lorenzo taunted.

"Come on, guys ... name your price," Cain pleaded.

Pete laughed and pushed the gun harder into Cain's flesh.

Officer Greg, having retrieved his gun from the ground, approached and took out a pair of handcuffs, snapping them on Cain's wrists. Lorenzo jerked Cain to his feet and handed him over to the police officer. "All yours," he said.

Alora struggled out of her mother's arms and ran to Bear, who was attempting to crawl his way to his young mistress. The child looked up at Jack, her eyes pleading for help. Jack got the message and knelt beside the wounded dog. He picked Bear up and turned to Heidi: "We need to get Bear to a vet. Greg will look after Cain."

Jack felt something moving around his legs and looked down. "Toby ... you did good, old man."

Toby flopped on the ground, exhaustion taking over. *Might be time to retire.* Toby gazed up at Jack, his eyes half-shut.

"Don't worry, old man. We'll be home soon and you can rest all you want. Right now, though, we need to get Bear to a vet, and I need to carry him, so he doesn't lose any more blood than necessary."

Toby meowed tiredly and struggled to his feet. *If I must, then. I'll walk. But when we get home, I expect perfect service, which means you'll be having to wait on me—paw and paw!*

Heidi noticed how tired Toby was and approached Jack, Alora right behind her. "I'll carry him, Jack," Heidi offered, and bending down, she scooped Toby up into her arms.

Lorenzo approached Jack. "Pete and I will be on our way. We left a lady and her two kids in our car. Hopefully, they're still there."

"Cameron's wife and children?" Jack asked.

"Yep."

"Okay." Jack paused. "What are your intentions, Lorenzo?"

"What do you mean?" A hint of tension was in Lorenzo's tone.

"Well, the way I see it, you and Pete could probably cut a deal with the court if you would be willing to testify against Cain," Jack commented, weighing his words carefully.

Lorenzo cleared his throat. "I'll deliver the lady to wherever she wants to go, and then Pete and I are out of here. Gone. With. The. Wind. The only reason we're still here is we needed to rescue Alora. Now she's safe—her and Heidi—we've done our job." He turned to Heidi. "It looks like you're in good hands now; you won't need me anymore." Not allowing for further conversation, Lorenzo motioned to Pete, and the two men were out of sight in no time.

Jack noticed the look of desolation on Heidi's face and knew what she was thinking; she was losing a valuable friend. "We need to go, Heidi," was all he could say. "We'll meet you back at the warehouse," Jack called over to Greg, who was on his cell phone while keeping a close eye on his prisoner.

46

Carrie was restless. She was tired of waiting for the two men who had rescued her and the kids and wasn't sure if she should wait for them to return. Her thoughts took her down the road of what-ifs. What if those men were still working for Cain? What if their real intention was to turn her over to that monster?

Gathering her courage, Carrie opened the car door.

Cameron decided to get as far away from Brantford as he could. He'd given up the one main account to Cain, but there was another one with enough money in it to sustain him for a time—at least until he found another source of income. The only thing he had to do was get back to his house, undetected, pack a bag, and grab the plane ticket he'd purchased.

Opening the car door, Cameron stepped out and took a deep breath. *Carrie and the kids will be better off without me; maybe, I'll send for them later. Maybe not.*

Cameron started walking on the gravel on the side of the road, heading back to Brantford. The way, so far, was void of cars. Suddenly, as he rounded a bend, Cameron noticed a woman and two children walking along the side of the road, just ahead of him. "Damn!" he cursed under his breath.

Carrie, being nervous, was continually checking behind her to ensure no one was following her. As she turned again, she saw Cameron. "Oh, my God!" Carrie screamed and started running toward him, Devlin and Cindy trying to keep up with their mother. "You son of a bitch!" Carrie shrieked when she reached her husband. She pummelled his chest with her fists. "How could you do what you did to this family?" She paused a moment and backed away. "Where are you going now, Cameron?" she asked, despite not really caring to know the answer.

Cameron hesitated. He had no desire to tell his wife the truth of what he was planning. His face blushed as he lied: "Home to wait for you, Carrie. I knew the police would rescue you…"

"The police! Ha! It wasn't the police who rescued us, Cameron. It was a couple of ex-criminals who saved our lives." No sooner were those words out of Carrie's mouth, Lorenzo and Pete drove up and stopped beside the ruined family.

Lorenzo rolled down his window and, resting his arm on the door, "Everything okay here?"

"Not your business, mister," Cameron retorted sarcastically.

Carrie spoke up immediately before Cameron could dig a deeper hole for her and the children. At this point, she didn't care what happened to her husband; Carrie's priority was her children and getting them home safely. "Stop, Cameron. These are the men who saved our lives." Leaning over and looking in the vehicle, "Everything is good here." A pause, as Carrie thought of something. "However, we could use a ride if you are heading back to Brantford. I'd like to go home, and it's a long walk, especially for the kids."

Lorenzo looked at Pete. This scenario didn't exactly mesh with their plans. When they hadn't found Carrie and the kids waiting for them in the car, they'd decided to just head straight to the airport and get out of the country.

Everything they needed was in the trunk, and their money was secure in an off-shore account.

Pete shrugged his shoulders: "Won't hurt, I guess. The police will be too busy booking Cain and his cronies to worry about us. But just the woman and kids," Pete added.

Cameron was furious at this turn of events. He watched his family drive away in a stranger's vehicle, and once again thought about just getting out of the country. *How can she be so callous? I was so right … gotta get out of here … but now Carrie is going to be at the house, how am I going to get what I need? Guess I'll just have to wait until she leaves somewhere and pray the cops don't track me down before my window of opportunity disappears.*

As Lorenzo's taillights disappeared, a caravan of police vehicles approached. Cameron was in no mood to be picked up by the police. He turned back into the woods––just in time.

47

When Jack arrived back at the warehouse, Bear in his arms, he went straight to Captain Wagner, who was standing beside his cruiser. One of the officers had brought it up to the warehouse for him. "Bryce, I need your car," Jack called out. "The dog took a bullet and I have to get him to the vet." Bryce didn't hesitate. He threw Jack the keys, then turned back to his business at hand—directing the loading up of prisoners to take back to the police station.

Heidi slipped in the front seat with Toby, still comfortably nestled in her arms, and Alora made her way to the backseat where Jack had laid Bear. Alora lifted the dog's head onto her lap and ran her hand softly over his head and down his back, whispering to her friend that he was going to be okay. Bear looked up at her with his pain-filled doggy eyes and let out a contented sigh.

48

Lorenzo and Pete dropped Carrie and her children off at their house, wished Carrie well, and then proceeded to the airport. “Time to get out of here before the cops change their minds and come after us,” Lorenzo said.

Pete chuckled. “Personally, I don’t think they give a rat’s ass about us. They’ve got Cain and his cronies to process. We’re the least of their worries.”

Two hours later, Lorenzo and Pete were on their way to Portugal with enough money to sustain them for a long time. On the way, they discussed opening a little eatery on the beach and hiring some locals to run it while they sat back and sipped cocktails on the deck of their beach house—once they renovated it, of course.

Kurt and Luigi had made their way to the road, coming to the edge of the woods just in time to flag down a transport truck.

“Where to, boys?” the driver asked.

Kurt spoke up before Luigi could say a word, having already thought of a plan. “Are you going anywhere near Brantford?” he asked.

“Not stopping in the city, but I can drop you off at the tourist centre on Gretzky Parkway if that will do.”

Kurt nodded. “That will do just fine.” Kurt knew the tourist centre wasn’t far from the Royal Bank on Lynden Road, which was where he had some money stashed in a safe-deposit box. From there, it would be easy enough to call a cab and head to the Toronto airport, book a flight and get out of town. They'd have to take a chance and go to their apartment to grab some clothes and their passports first.

An hour later, Kurt and Luigi were coming out of the apartment building and about to get into a cab when they heard the police sirens. Kurt leaned over the front seat: "Move it, man. There's an extra $50 for you if you get us out of here."

The cabbie's face paled; the last thing he needed was trouble. The driver shook his head back and forth. "Don't want any trouble, man."

Kurt, who was in the front seat, pulled out his gun and levelled it at the man's stomach. "You'll be getting more than trouble if you don't move the car!" he snapped.

The cabbie put his hands up in the air. "Look, man. Just take my cab. Do whatever you want with it. Just let me go … please … I have a family … a wife … children … please."

Luigi didn't like what his partner was doing. "Come on, Kurt, just let the guy out. He said we could have the cab."

The sound of police sirens was getting closer and the flashing lights soon became visible. Kurt made a quick decision. Opening the car door, he reached in the back and grabbed his bag. "Okay, Luigi. Let's go. We'll find another way out of the city. We're going to need to lay low for a few hours. Once thc cops know we aren't here, they'll give up. It sure didn't take Cain long to give up the locations of people who dedicated their lives to do his dirty work."

But it was too late. Two cruisers screeched to a stop, and four officers got out with guns pointed at Kurt and Luigi. "Bags down … hands on the trunk of the cab," one of the officers ordered.

Mitch was preparing to board his flight to Cuba when he noticed two police officers approaching. “Damn!” he cursed under his breath. Mitch tried hard to ignore them, gripping his gym bag and moving forward to the boarding desk. Too late. A hand gripped his arm.

“Are you Mitch Johnson?” one of the police officers questioned.

Mitch thought of denying. After all, his passport had another name on it, and he could get away. But then, Mitch saw the photo in the other officer’s hand. *Damn! I knew I should have disguised!* Mitch had wanted to dye his hair and put on a fake moustache but had gotten anxious, feeling his time to get away was running short. He would have been able to explain the hair colour difference by merely telling the clerk he’d dyed his hair.

Finally, making his decision, Mitch nodded. His thoughts were running like a torrential river, thinking how he could maybe talk his way out of prison if he told the cops everything he knew about Cain.

“No need to cuff me, officer,” Mitch suggested. “I’ll come with you willingly.”

The officer grinned. “Sorry, Mitch. Protocol.”

Half an hour later, Mitch was sitting in an interrogation room, spilling his guts about his old boss. The District Attorney didn’t promise him as much leniency as Mitch had hoped.

“You’ll have to serve your time for murdering Sam Sicarello,” the DA informed. “There’s also the issue of Carrie MacPherson and her children, and blowing up a property with the attempt to hide evidence.”

“Come on, man. Give me a break.” Mitch acted cocky, despite the anxiety he was feeling. “I was acting on orders from Cain Lawson." Mitch leaned as far forward as his restraints would allow. "I'll give you everything I know about the man, but only if you give me a little something." He leaned back in his chair.

The DA studied Mitch for a moment. As badly as he wanted to put the scum sitting in front of him in prison for the rest of Mitch's miserable life, the DA wanted Cain more. "Okay, let me hear what you have to say and I will do something for you in return." The DA paused, noting the victory look that crossed through Mitch's eyes. "But not scot-free."

Mitch grinned, knowing that after he revealed the extent of what he knew about Cain, his sentence would be drastically reduced. When his sentence was handed down––fifteen years, with the chance of parole after ten—Mitch calculated how much interest his money in the island account would have earned. And he would only be forty if he got out after the ten years. *I guess it will be best behaviour for me for a while and then easy street for the rest of my life!*

Cameron decided he had only one viable option. There was no way he was going to desert his family, and after he talked to Carrie, Cameron turned himself back into the police. He would still have to serve some time, but if he turned evidence on Cain and his gang, the prosecutor would reduce his sentence. He took the deal—two years less a day, which he'd serve as community service.

Bear spent a week at the vet's, and when he got home, although he wasn't fully back to his usual bouncy self, the dog's tail never stopped wagging. Toby and Jack visited Bear, and Heidi had special treats ready for Toby. Ever since he'd saved the day, knocking the gun out of Cain's hand, Heidi hadn't been able to do enough for the old orange feline detective. Plus, much to Toby's chagrin, Alora had lavished gobs of attention on Toby, even making her way every morning over to Jack's to give her saviour a multitude of hugs!

Epilogue

Toby stood up on the back of the couch and stretched. It had been a long couple of months, but finally, Cain's trial started. The judge had denied him bail— Cain was a definite flight risk. The judge realized Heidi and Alora could be at risk if the man were free until his trial. Jack kept Toby appraised of the case, and it wasn't long before the trial was over. Cain received twenty-five years with no chance of parole.

The day the verdict came down, Jack, Tessa, and Toby, along with Heidi, Alora, and Bear, went out to celebrate. Heidi and Tessa packed a picnic lunch, and the entourage trekked down to the Grand River and found a quiet spot on the bank.

"So, now what?" Jack asked, taking a sip of his juice. "Do you plan to move on now Cain is in jail … start over somewhere else?"

Heidi thought for a moment. "I'd like to, but I wouldn't mind staying here in Brantford, either. Alora likes it here. She loves Toby. And where could I find a better place than this with such a large yard for the price I'm paying here." Heidi paused. "I've thought about going back to work, especially with Alora in school now. She's made some friends, and I think there's been enough trauma in her life to last her a lifetime! She needs roots."

Jack nodded and smiled.

Tessa spoke up: "I think that's an excellent idea, Heidi." Then, pointing to where Toby and Bear, snoozing under a tree, "and I think Toby would miss you guys if you were to move," she added with a light chuckle.

Toby opened his eyes for a second, then blinked them shut. *Not on your life, Tessa! Wouldn't miss them for a second!* Toby nestled closer to Bear and sighed deeply. Bear put a protective paw around Toby and wagged his tail.

Meanwhile, in another city…

Emma was just coming back from a run and heard the phone ringing. She recognized the number on the call display—the prison where Camden, her brother, was incarcerated.

"Hello," she answered.

"Is this Emma Gale?" the voice on the other end of the line asked.

"Yes." Emma felt a strange sensation crawl through the pit of her stomach.

"It's about your brother, Camden. We need you to come down to the prison as soon as possible."

Emma dropped the receiver, grabbed her car keys, and raced out the door. Bursting into the front office of the prison, Emma raced up to the reception desk. "I'm here about my brother, Camden Gale," she informed.

The woman looked down at her desk, and her lips formed an 'O' before she reached over and buzzed Emma through the security door. She stood. "Follow me." Within a couple of minutes, the woman was knocking on the warden's office door.

"Come in," ordered a gruff voice from the other side.

When Emma was alone with the warden, she once again began to feel sick to her stomach.

"I have some bad news for you, Emma," the warden began. "Your brother, Camden, committed suicide two hours ago."

Emma leaned over the desk, getting right in the warden's face. "How did you let this happen? How did it happen?!' she screamed angrily.

The warden explained how Camden had been sinking deeper into depression, and they had been trying out a new medication on him. "He seemed to be improving," the warden informed, "but the psychiatrist brought it to my attention yesterday that he was worried Camden might be regressing again and suggested we put him on suicide watch."

"Did you?" Emma demanded angrily.

"Not yet. We were short-staffed this morning, a couple guards calling in sick." The warden looked away from the eyes piercing into his.

Emma turned slowly and started to leave the room. At the door, she looked back for a moment: "Let me know when I can have my brother's remains picked up."

The warden nodded.

Emma drove home, unhurriedly. Her tears came slowly at first, but by the time she arrived at her apartment, they were flowing in a torrent of grief.

Duke, her dog, greeted her at the door; he sensed something wrong with his mistress and pushed his nose gently on her hand.

"He's gone, Duke. Camden's gone, and I don't know what to do. I have nobody now." Emma made her way to the living room and flopped on the couch. Duke sat in front of her and waited for Emma to make her next move.

Finally, after about half an hour, Emma reached for the phone and dialled the number of the only friend she felt she had. The only friend she thought cared about her.

"Hello," the familiar voice came through the receiver.

"Jack..."

"Emma?"

"I need you, Jack. Camden's gone!"

Toby perked up when he heard Jack say, 'Emma.' He jumped off the couch and walked to where Jack was sitting, talking on the phone. Toby sat down and waited.

"Gone?" Jack put the phone on speaker so Toby could hear the conversation.

"He committed suicide."

"I'm so sorry, Emma."

"I'd like to come back to Brantford. You're the only other person I know..." Emma began hesitantly, not knowing how Jack would receive this request. She sensed he hadn't been too sure about her innocence when she was on trial for hurting that man. Fortunately for her, he hadn't been able to identify her.

"Someone's living in the house now, Emma," Jack informed. He paused. "I suppose you could stay here with Toby and me until you find something else."

Emma sighed. When she spoke, her voice sounded tearful: "Thank you, Jack. You have no idea how much I appreciate your kindness right now. I have no one else," she re-emphasized.

"I'll bring my truck down tomorrow and help you move your belongings here." A pause. "Have you made any arrangements for Camden?"

"No. I have no idea where to begin," came the tearful reply.

"Okay, I'll call a funeral home here in town and get something arranged for you. See you tomorrow." Jack hung up the phone and looked at Toby. "I guess your Emma is coming to stay with us for a while, old man."

Toby was ecstatic he'd be seeing Emma again. But, Toby knew what his friend was capable of—what she'd done.

Oh, Emma, I'm sorry that Camden's gone, and it's my biggest hope that you've changed. But, I've got a sinking feeling that…

Toby slipped out his cat door, heading out for a walk. He needed time to think. As he passed Heidi's place, he noticed Alora and Bear in the backyard.

Good thing Heidi has no idea what Emma did in the basement of the house she's living in. He continued on his way, heading to the park near his home. *Oh, Emma. It'll be good to see you again, but…*

A tear slipped out of the corner of Toby's eye.

A Peek at some of

Detective Toby's

Other Adventures...

Are You Listening to Me?

MARY M. CUSHNIE-MANSOUR

PREFACE:

It's been a while since my last big case, so I will jog your memory about who I am. My name is Toby, and I live with Jack Nelson, a retired cop. I used to be quite stout, but since venturing into police work, I have put myself on a rigorous routine of fitness and healthy eating. That doesn't always work out for me because, as my nature dictates, I am inclined to be a tad lazy sometimes—most of the time, actually. And I never miss a meal or a snack if I am passing through the kitchen. My hair is red; I once heard someone say redheads were God's chosen people, so I assume that goes for cats too.

Now do you remember? Yes, I am a cat—Detective Toby. I solved a crime about six months ago when Jack's friend went loony and kidnapped his own kids. I saw through him right from the beginning; Jack didn't. If it hadn't been for me, goodness knows what would have happened to those kids. I was a hero, and everyone was grateful to me. The police department awarded me with a framed certificate, which certified I was a 'Class-A Detective.' I was told I was welcome any time down at the police station, which I take full advantage of every time Jack visits the captain, Bryce Wagner.

There have been a lot of changes in the past six months. Jack renovated the back door. I now have my own special cat door so I can come and go from the house as I please. Jack figured if another crime needed investigating, I wouldn't have to wait for someone to open the door to get out and about detectiving if I had my own. There have also been some significant changes on the street. The old gym that used to be owned by Mardy Hampton was sold, and the new owners tore down the old building and are constructing a new one. I heard Jack say they were hoping to have it up and running by early spring. Jack has been talking about getting out of the neighbourhood for a time because he can't sleep well with all the banging going on. Personally, I can sleep through most anything, but the 24-hour noise is starting to get to me, too.

At first, I thought Jack was going to move us completely out of the neighbourhood, but was relieved when I saw him just packing for a camping trip in his old campervan. I knew he wouldn't leave me behind since I accompanied him most places now. I won't bore you with the details of our month-long excursion through Northern Ontario because it isn't relevant to the story that is going to unfold in the pages to follow.

Enough introductions. You know who I am now and you will be hearing more from me as the story of what happened during the summer of 2009 on the street where I live unfolds.

...

Saturday, May 16, 2009

Camden stood. "Well, Doctor—Lucy," he dared to call her, thinking, what the heck, it was probably the last time he would ever see her. He extended his hand. "I guess this is it. Thanks again for your time and for all you've done for me. You're better than most." He smiled again.

Doctor Hatfield took his offered hand and shook it. His fingers were cold. She looked into his eyes and saw the iciness there and wondered if she shouldn't try harder to follow through on exactly where he was going and if he was really going to be doing what he said he was. The story of getting a job at a new gym fell in with the kinds of jobs he had held in the past, and with his current one. But lately Camden had voiced lots of dissatisfaction with working there. He had complained that most of the clientele were phoney at the best of times and that he felt they didn't appreciate him for all he did for them. He'd even gone so far as to blame some of them for a couple of the reprimands he had received. It was in the moments he was sharing such information that Doctor Hatfield saw his darkness the most.

"Good luck, Camden. Keep in touch ... I mean that."

Camden smiled—stiff and deliberate. "Sure, doctor, I'll make a point to do that." He turned and walked out of the office.

He didn't bother to acknowledge the secretary. If only he had a bit longer in Vancouver, he would show her. But things were closing in on him—heating up—he needed to move on. All there was left to do was go home and tell Emma. At least this time he had everything in place ahead of time. He had a job and had rented a house just down the street from where he would be working. He had seen pictures of the house. It would be perfect for Emma and her plants, with its three-season room attached to the kitchen.

Doctor Hatfield asked her secretary to hold off before sending in the next patient. He wasn't due for another half hour. She returned to her desk, pulled out Camden's full file, and opened it to the beginning notes—notes that were not hers—information she had managed to gather about him from other places where he had lived.

February 2006: notes on a new patient, Camden Gale ... patient very agitated when admitted to hospital ... admitted himself. He was under the delusion someone was out to get him—actually, several people. Camden works at a local gym doing odd jobs: cleaning, front desk, and serving drinks to the clients when other employees are on their breaks. Upon first sight, he appears to be quite normal and during most of our sessions, he is. Odd living situation, though—lives with his sister. Asked about meeting with her but he refused to allow such a visit, mentioning his sister had been through enough. I never managed to find out what that was. Camden was only my patient for a couple of months, he just stopped coming. I found out later he had moved to Calgary when a colleague of mine contacted me, asking for some advice. He was dealing with a troubled young man who had been admitted to the hospital. When I asked the name, and found out it was Camden Gale, I shared what I could. I forwarded him any notes and information I had on Camden, which wasn't a lot. We both agreed, on the surface, Camden possibly suffered from paranoia brought on by illusions of mistreatment, and misconceptions people were out to get him all the time...

Doctor Hatfield read through the rest of the notes, sorry she hadn't done so as thoroughly before. It might have saved some time, but she always liked to start fresh with her clients and not have a tainted view of them from other doctors. She made a note to give Doctor Morgan a call and moved on to the next set of records in the file.

April 2007: today I met the new fellow, whom a colleague told me about. He had not been able to take him on, saying he was already weighed down with cases. After a few sessions with Camden Gale, I had the feeling there was more to the good doctor's decision than work overload. On the surface, Camden appears quite normal. However, when certain buttons are pushed, such as discussing issues to do with family and work, he becomes agitated and irritable—paranoid that everyone is out to get him. I finally managed to find out he felt he had been neglected by his parents while growing up. In fact, upon deeper research, I discovered he and his sister, Emma, whom he lives with, were in foster care for several years. After our fifth session, I concluded that Camden Gale is paranoid delusional…

…

Tuesday, May 19, 2009

Jack had driven all night to get home. It had been great to get away from all the confusion, but he was looking forward to crawling into his queen-size bed and stretching his limbs to their fullest. He could tell Toby was happy to be heading home, as well.

"What do you say, old boy, shall we send out for a fish dinner for lunch?"

Toby looked up at Jack, meowed and licked his chops. Jack reached across the seat and scratched Toby behind the ears. "I'll take that as a yes."

As they pulled onto their street, the first thing they both noticed was that the gym was completed. There was a sign out front announcing the grand opening. "Times are changing, old boy," Jack pointed out.

Toby raced to the van window as he and Jack passed by Miss Mildred's house. *"What's that van doing in her driveway?"* he wondered. *"I'll check it out later while Jack is unpacking our stuff. There are benefits to being a cat—all the luxury without having to do any of the work."*

Jack stopped in front of his house and then backed the van into the driveway. He got out and waited for Toby to jump down. He thought it was strange how Toby had taken to the outdoors after all the years of being an inside cat. Toby headed down the street to Miss Mildred's.

"Don't you be gone long now, Toby. I don't want you to miss your fish lunch," Jack called after the disappearing tail.

Toby paid no attention. He was on a mission. He slunk up to the old wire fence that meandered around Miss Mildred's yard. *"What the heck is that? Miss Mildred doesn't have a dog!"* Toby saw Duke lying in the middle of the yard. Then he noticed the girl kneeling by the flowerbed. *"Maybe someone has come over to help her fix things up."*

The girl was humming. It was a melodic sound, yet mournful. Toby observed how pretty she was, and frail. Her long strawberry-blonde hair swept the grass. Toby moved closer to the fence for a better look. Duke's ears pricked forward. Toby stopped. The last thing he wanted was that great hulk of a dog charging at him when nothing but a flimsy wire fence separated them. Duke growled.

"What's the matter, Duke?" Emma looked up.

Duke stood and trotted over to Emma. He lay down protectively at her side, still growling. Emma patted his head. "Have you had enough of the outdoors, Duke?" She checked her watch. "Oh, it's lunch time already. I wonder where Camden is. Oh, I remember, he went to look at the gym, but that was an hour ago." She stood. "Well, he should be back for lunch; shall we go in and make him some?"

Toby kept very still as the girl and the dog moved across the yard to the back door. He noticed all the plants in Miss Mildred's three-season room; they hadn't been there before. *"Something really strange is going on here,"* Toby thought as he turned around and headed for home. *"No sense missing out on a good fish lunch, though."*

When Toby arrived home, Jack hadn't even started lunch. Toby could tell because he could smell fish a mile away on a rainy day. Jack was sitting on the front step talking to a strange young man. Toby climbed the steps, sat down and glared at Jack, who paid him no attention. Toby meowed.

"Hey there, old man," Jack finally noticed Toby.

"I wish you would quit 'old manning' me! I have a name, Jack. You wouldn't like it if I kept calling you old man, would you?" Toby stared at the young visitor.

"Toby, this is our new neighbour, Camden. He and his sister have moved into Miss Mildred's old place. Unfortunately, while we were gone, she passed away. Camden, this is my cat, Toby," Jack introduced.

Toby circled around on the porch, eyeing Camden. Camden was eye-balling Toby. *"Something wrong with this fellow. Don't like what I see behind those eyes!"* Toby prided himself on reading people.

"Does the cat really understand when you speak to him? It isn't like he's going to remember my name or anything." Camden's statement caused Jack to raise his eyebrows, but then he laughed.

"Oh, Toby understands more than you might think. He's a very smart cat. Actually solved a crime about six months ago and was awarded an honorary detective certificate," Jack explained.

Camden stared at Toby. "You don't say. Well, my sister and I will sleep much better knowing how protected our new neighbourhood is." He laughed and then checked his watch. "Wow, I didn't realize it was lunchtime. Emma will be worried." He stood and extended a hand to Jack. "It was nice meeting you, always good to know your neighbours."

"Likewise," Jack said as he shook Camden's hand. "Come around anytime. Bring your sister."

"Will do. Emma doesn't go out much, though." Camden stooped over to pet Toby.

Toby arched his back and hissed. *"Don't you be touchin' me!"* Toby raced to the door and meowed.

"Looks like your cat doesn't like me," Camden pointed out to Jack.

"You bet my paws, I don't!"

"Oh, Toby just gets a little cantankerous sometimes," Jack chuckled. "You'll get used to him."

"No, he won't!" Toby hissed again.

MARY M. CUSHNIE-MANSOUR

Running Away From Loneliness

Chapter One

Some things in life are worse than loneliness. Everyone around you thinking that all is good in your life—that you are a rock they can come to, to pour out their troubles to, that you will fix everything with a smile and an assurance all will be well in their lives and in the world—*that* is worse than loneliness.

Such a person was Violet Saunders, but she had finally come to a breaking point. She was tired of being there for everyone else. She was tired of trying to fix everything for the people around her. She was tired of not having the moments to herself she longed for, for so many years—for too many years. She was just plain tired of her lonely life.

…

Violet wandered into the room she'd set up as an office and ran her fingers over the keyboard of her laptop. The laptop held all her poetry and stories. It kept her secrets, secrets she didn't want anyone to find out, which is why she'd password protected her computer. Even Frank didn't know the password. She sat down in her office chair and turned it to face the window. It was raining outside. She picked up a pen and tapped it on her desk. She was lonely. Lonelier than ever she had been. Her life was busy, but it was a life spent looking after others, listening to others' problems, and trying to pursue her dream amid everything else. Violet stood, a grimly-defined firmness to her jaw. She knew what was required—to save herself.

…

Jack Nelson, a retired cop who lived with his oversized orange tabby, Toby, was tired. He needed a break from the everyday routine. The Camden Gale case had drained him mentally, especially when Toby was recovering from the injuries he'd sustained saving the final victim of Camden's scourge, Jack's friend, Andrew.

Camden Gale murdered five people because he thought they'd insulted him in some way or another. Camden's sister, Emma, had needed Jack's emotional support when her brother, the only family she had, was sent off to prison.

But Toby was wholly recovered now and Emma seemed to be managing on her own quite well. Jack decided he and Toby should take a short, but well-earned, vacation. He knew of a quiet little lake up in the Kingston, Ontario area, and had a friend who owned several cottages there. The cottages were spread far apart so Jack could be assured of peace and quiet.

…

Toby found Jack busy putting the last of the supplies into the camper. "Hey there, old man, have a nice visit with Emma?"

You bet. Toby sat in the driveway and began grooming his fur as he watched Jack finish loading the camper.

"I'll be back in a sec," Jack began. "I think it's wise to let Emma know we'll be away for a couple weeks, maybe ask her to keep an eye on our place … pick up my mail and paper, too."

Good man, Jack. I was hoping you'd do that. Toby headed to the house, and his dish.

~

Early the next morning, Jack and Toby left for their quiet vacation on a remote lake in the Kingston area.

…

A week after Violet made the decision to do something about her life, she was driving along a country road toward a cabin she'd rented just outside Kingston, Ontario. Her mind wandered over the events of the past few days, to the working out of her plan. Violet felt guilty for leaving the way she had, but hopefully, in the long run, she would be able to repair any damage she might have inflicted on her relationship with her husband. She'd left Frank a letter explaining why. She had faith he would understand and give her the time she needed. She hoped, anyway.

The song on the radio finished and the newscast started with the breaking story of an escaped killer from the Kingston penitentiary.

Great, just what I need, an escaped killer to add some excitement to my life!

…

Syd Lance couldn't believe his luck, having escaped the two lazy—in his opinion—guards who had been transporting him to the hospital in Kingston for a procedure that couldn't be done at the prison hospital. He had told them he needed to use the restroom to take a piss and a shit, his condition worsening, he'd said. They'd pulled into a gas station, seen him to the bathroom, removed his chains, and waited outside the door.

The idiots hadn't thought to check for a window, which Syd thought was a bit off, especially for George. George had a bad reputation around the facility for being a hard-ass; Larry, on the other hand, was new to the prison and Syd hadn't seen him before. Syd could hear them laughing and joking outside the door and was thankful for their noise—it made it a lot easier for him in case there was any unforeseen sounds involved with what he was about to do.

Having worked out every day in his cell, Syd was as fit as he could be and small in stature—small enough to slip through the undersized window in the washroom. As he fiddled with the window, trying to get it open, one of the guards—sounded like George—knocked on the door and asked how he was doing.

"Doing okay … ahhh … shouldn't be long … stomachs just … ahhh!" Syd replied, as the window finally opened for him.

Standing on the back of the toilet, Syd squeezed his body through the opening. Fortunately, the drop to the ground was not far and he quickly found his footing and took off to the wooded area behind the station. He was deep in the woods before he heard the siren and knew he was going to have to pick up his pace and get somewhere that he wouldn't be found.

…

Toby was restless, unable to sleep. He was thinking to blame it on Jack giving him nothing more than dry kibble for supper, not the fresh fish he'd been expecting. He jumped off the end of the bed where he'd been trying to catch some sleep and wandered into the main room of the cottage.

Noticing an open window minus a screen, Toby jumped up onto the sill and stared out into the darkness. The night sounds were soft in the distance—crickets and frogs. A rustling in the nearby trees drew Toby's attention. He narrowed his eyes in that direction. *Shouldn't be leaving windows open, Jack. Don't like thinking someone could just come in while we're sleeping and knock us off!* Toby jumped down onto the porch.

He moved silently across the yard to where the sounds had come from. *While you're sleeping away, Jack, I'll keep an eye on things for you—one of us needs to be on the job.*

As Toby approached the edge of the woods, he paused as another rustling hit his ears. *Maybe this wasn't such a good idea, coming out here in the pitch dark. Might have been safer at the foot of the bed. At least that way, if someone was going to attack us, they'd get Jack first—he's a larger target, and despite my slight over-weightiness, I can still get under the bed!*

Toby waited a few more seconds, listening intently for more rustling, however, all was quiet except for the crickets and frogs. *Must have been a false alarm. No sense freezing the fur off my toes out here.* He turned and made his way back to the cabin, jumped through the open window, and headed to the bed. As he nestled back into the covers, Jack groaned and changed positions. The night air must have made Toby sleepy because he was snoring within minutes.

Past Ghosts

MARY M. CUSHNIE-MANSOUR

Prologue

Emma had taken to jogging around town regularly, Duke, her dog, always accompanying her. Usually, her route would take her through downtown Brantford, and many times, she would veer off the sidewalks and hit the trails, especially the ones running along the Grand River. She'd also taken to hanging out at various parks in the central part of the city. Some of the incidents she witnessed were appalling.

With each unsavoury incident Emma witnessed, the rage inside her escalated. The need to do something about it became more urgent. Within the past two weeks, Emma had observed four abusive situations where a guy was pushing his girlfriend around aggressively or screaming verbal abuse at them. Red lights flashed before Emma's eyes each time until her wrath was so deep-seated that she knew she had to do something to stop the onslaught of abuses.

Life wasn't the same without her brother, Camden, who was serving a life sentence for murdering several people. At times, Emma felt life was better, though. She could be herself. She didn't have to act the fragile female—well, not within the confines of her four walls, that is. To the outside world, to her friends, Jack and Toby, she still needed to keep up the façade of the weak female.

There was nothing weak about Emma. She'd been training for a long time, building her strength and her fighting skills. Even Camden hadn't known the extent of what she was doing. After he was incarcerated, Emma purchased a punching bag and set it up in the basement, escalating her training. She felt ready now—as prepared as she was ever going to be.

Emma began researching online drugs she could procure to help with the mission she was about to embark on. Not medications for herself, but ones to administrate to the vile creatures that deemed it their privilege to abuse women.

Emma came across the drug, Rohypnol. It was a tranquillizer said to be ten times more potent than valium and said to impair the memory. Reading on, she discovered it caused loss of muscle control, confusion, and made a person drowsy. Emma smiled when she read the line about Rohypnol's street name being *roofie* and that it was used as a date rape drug. So perfect for her upcoming mission.

Emma read several accounts of female victims having been sexually assaulted at parties after having had a drink. Many of them described their inability to move and stop what was being done to them, and later, when the drug wore off, their memories were impaired and they could not recall what had happened to them.

"This sounds like just what I need to teach abusive men a lesson," Emma mumbled as she searched Google how to obtain the drug. "I know you're illegal in Canada and the United States, but guys must be getting it from somewhere..."

Several sources showed up in the feed. "Well, well..." The grin on her face was broad as she sat forward and clicked the link to a source in Mexico.

"Expensive," Emma grumbled as she got up and went to her dresser to get a credit card from her wallet. "But going to be oh so worth it! Using this stuff, I'll be able to teach these guys a lesson, let them go, and they won't remember what happened to them—or who did it to them!"

Emma turned her computer off and walked downstairs for some breakfast. Duke stood to attention when she entered the kitchen, his tail wagging a greeting.

"Need to go out for a few minutes, boy?" Emma pushed the sliding door to the three-season room across and proceeded to the outer door, Duke close on her heels. "There you go, Duke," she said, letting him out into the yard.

As Emma prepared a protein drink for her breakfast, she felt the blood palpitating through her veins, the heat of it flushing her usually pale skin. Emma sipped her drink, thinking what her next move was to be. Before she did anything concrete, she'd have to wait for the Rohypnol to arrive.

Finishing her drink, Emma rinsed her cup and left it in the sink. She gazed out to the yard; Duke was laying in the shade under a big maple. She smiled, comforted by the sight of her faithful companion.

"Time for a workout," Emma said, checking her watch. "Then, Duke and I will go hunting."

About the Author

Mary M. Cushnie-Mansour resides in Brantford, ON, Canada. She is the award-winning author of the popular "Night's Vampire" series. Mary has a freelance journalism certificate from Waterloo University, and in the past, she wrote a short story column and feature articles for the Brantford Expositor. She has also published collections of poetry and short-story anthologies, youth novels, bilingual children's books, English children's story books, and a biography.

Mary has always believed in encouraging people's imaginations and spent several years running the "Just Imagine" program for the local school board. She has also been heavily involved in the local writing community, inspiring adults to follow their dreams. Mary is available for speaking engagements and writing workshops for children and adults.

You can contact Mary through her website
http://www.writerontherun.ca
or via email
mary@writerontherun.ca

Manufactured by Amazon.ca
Bolton, ON

37275536R00149